USA TODAY BESTSELLING AUTHOR
ERIN BEDFORD

UNTIL DAWN

Also by Erin Bedford

The Underground Series
Chasing Rabbits
Chasing Cats
Chasing Princes
Chasing Shadows
Chasing Hearts
The Crimes of Alice
Hatter's Heart

The Mary Wiles Chronicles
Marked by Hell
Bound by Hell
Deceived by Hell
Tempted by Hell

Starcrossed Dragons
Riding Lightning
Grinding Frost
Swallowing Fire
Pounding Earth

The Crimson Fold
Until Midnight
Until Dawn
Until Sunset

Curse of the Fairy Tales
Rapunzel Untamed
Rapunzel Unveiled
Rapunzel Unchained

Her Angels

Heaven's Embrace
Heaven's A Beach
Heaven's Most Wanted

<u>House of Durand</u>
Indebted to the Vampires
Wanted by the Vampires
Protected by the Vampires
Embrace of the Vampires
Tempted by the Butler
Loved by the Vampires
Huntress of the Vampires

<u>Academy of Witches</u>
Witching On A Star
As You Witch
Witch You Were Here
Just Witch It
Summer Witchin'

<u>Children of the Fallen</u>
Death In Her Eyes
Fire In Her Blood

The Beast of the Fae Court
Granting Her Wish
Vampire CEO

ERIN BEDFORD

UNTIL DAWN

Chapter 1

THE VIEW FROM MY new room was even better than my old one. Not only could I see the whole of the Inner Circle, but I could see the edges of the Glade as well.

I hated it.

Ever since the election, a growing sense of dread had filled me. Sure, to the outsider, I was living the dream, a little nobody from the Glade having moved up the ladder all the way up to the top. I had servants and fine clothes. The food was above par. I even had friends there to help me through the transition.

But I'd never felt more alone.

I turned my attention away from the fabulous view to my new room. Patrick, the leader of all of Alban and head of the Crimson Fold, had insisted my room be moved closer to his. I wasn't sure if that was for my comfort or so he could keep a better eye on me. Either way, it was better than the alternative.

Many of the elected, those who had been chosen as companions to the great members of the Crimson Fold, didn't get shiny new rooms with four-poster beds covered in deep red silk sheets. No, they didn't even get their own bedroom, not by my friend Violet's account.

A small girl who I had become quick friends with during the whole election process, Violet had almost died during that process. Still, somehow, she ended up being chosen by one of the best of the Fold members. I wouldn't call her situation the best though.

Apparently, companions could be anything the Fold members wanted. Friend, slave, lover, willing or not. Violet had assured me that Maleria hadn't forced herself on her, but she did make Violet sleep in her bed.

I shuddered at the thought of sleeping in Patrick's bed, and I couldn't tell if it was from revulsion or excitement. My keeper, as I had come to call him, was an enigma for sure. With his pale hair and pale eyes, he had me questioning whether or not I wanted to bring him closer or shove a stake through his heart.

Not that I knew if that would even kill him. He was a monster, they all were, and if Patrick had his way, I'd be one too before the week's end.

My thoughts were interrupted by a knock on my door. I snorted at the false show of courtesy. They might knock, but I didn't let myself believe for a minute that they wouldn't barge in without my consent. I was a prisoner, not a guest or even a resident, as they would like me to believe.

I snorted again as I turned my back to the door, not bothering to let them in. They'd come in or they wouldn't.

The door clicked open behind me, and a scoff followed by an exasperated sigh told me only one person could have entered.

"You're still not dressed? It's already noon." Asher's voice held an amount of irritation that I didn't bother to acknowledge.

Asher had been my guide, was now in charge of my wardrobe, and one of the only people in this hell hole disguised as a palace that I could trust. Or at least I used to trust. That was before I found out he was also one of the monsters.

"If I want to sleep all day, then I will. Not like I had anything better to do." I flopped down on my bed, which to my utter dissatisfaction felt like a cloud. If I were going to be a prisoner, it would only make sense for the bed too hard and the room cold.

"Sure, you do." Asher rounded the bed to stand over me, his long hair hanging over his face. "You could be preparing for your conversion. Getting to know the other members of the Fold. Or maybe even getting to know Patrick better." He raised a brow at me, and I scowled.

Patrick might be an enigma I wanted to unravel, but that didn't mean I would willingly spend time with him if I didn't have to. He and Asher had been lying to me from the start, and since I couldn't exactly rebuff Asher who had a way of not being ignored, Patrick was getting the brunt of my anger.

Asher shrugged off my look of disdain as he adjusted his own appearance in one of my many mirrors. "Either way, your absence was noticed at breakfast this morning, and while I'm sure they are giving you time to get acquainted with your new life, don't think for a second that they will leave you be for long." He gave me a pointed look that made me shift on the bed. "Eventually, they will expect you to play your part, whether you want to or not."

"And what part would that be?" I sat up on my elbows. "The one that you and Patrick concocted or the one the Fold thinks I'm to play? Because really I'm getting a bit confused here."

Letting out a frustrated sigh, Asher sat on the bed next to me. "I know we are asking a lot of you, but I thought you wanted to help your people, those back in the Glade that work day and night to get meager scraps from the capital? Or did you forget about them already in your determination to get back at Patrick and I for lying to you?"

"Of course, I haven't." I shot up to a seated position, my brow furrowed. "I still want to help everyone. It's not right they are in the dark about what's going on up here, as well as the suffering. Don't think I'm just going to play the perfect part and not make sure to expose the Fold for what they really are." I glared at him like he was going to rebuff me at any moment, chastising me like a child wearing pants too big for them.

"And we don't expect you to." Asher patted my hand with a reassuring smile. "We want you to do exactly that, but more subtly than just shouting it from the streets. That's a sure-fire way to get yourself wiped or worse killed."

I frowned at Asher's mention of being wiped. I'd met a few who'd had their memory wiped, and most of them were a bit simple in the head. Even more so when it has happened on multiple occasions to someone, like with Tillie. I didn't want anyone poking around inside of my head for any reason.

"So, what do I do then?" I sighed, staring down at my feet. "Just pretend everything is fine until you and Patrick deem to let me know what the plan is?" I cocked a brow at him and then shook my head. "No offense, but I don't want to be like you, no matter the benefits."

My eyes strayed to the book I still had on my nightstand, *A Guide for the Newly Converted.* Over the last few days, I had scoured the book for any and everything I could find out about being turned into a vampire, all the downfalls and the benefits. And while the bloodlust and the sensitivity to light weren't the worse negatives, the longevity seemed worse to me.

Who wanted to live forever? Watch all your friends and family die while you stayed young and beautiful forever?

Sounded more like a curse than a blessing to me.

"It's not as bad as you would think," Asher tried to reassure me with a wry grin. "If you would give it a chance, you might just like the new you. I know I hated the person I was before I was turned." Asher's eyes darkened as he was caught up in some thought. Though I knew that Patrick had turned Asher, I didn't know much more about the mysterious guide. Asher was about as much of an enigma as his cousin. Would I be that way once I was changed?

If I was changed, I corrected myself.

Snorting at my own thoughts, I turned back to Asher. "I like how I am now, thank you very much." Though that was a bit of a lie. My hair was too dull of a brown and my eyes too colorless to be pretty. I had a good frame, but I'd never be called a great beauty. Not like my step sisters.

Thinking of Lea and Julianna made me even more depressed. They were probably living it up now that I had won the election. I hadn't gotten to see them recently, but I could imagine they have moved out of their large home into an even bigger one. They probably had new servants and were lording it up to all their classmates. I hoped at least my father was keeping some perspective.

My father's insistence for me to leave right before the finale of the election made my stomach twist into knots. Someone had put him up to it. Someone who didn't want me here, and I had no doubt that it had something to do with Zara. That nasty piece of work had landed a companion position, and would no doubt be taking every chance to make my life a living hell while in the Core.

All the more reason to get out of here, I told myself.

"Well," - Asher clapped his hands together and stood from the bed - "you might like you, but I think everyone would agree with me when I tell you that you smell ripe." He pinched his nose in obvious disgust.

I wrinkled my brow. I didn't smell that bad. Sure, I'd wallowed in my room for the last few days. I hadn't bothered to shower, I wasn't seeing anyone. In the Glade, we went weeks without showering. I didn't see the big deal.

I tilted my head down and gave my armpit a testing sniff. Ugh. Okay, maybe I did need a shower.

"Alright, dear, enough self-pity. Time to face the world." Asher offered me a hand, and I begrudgingly took it, letting myself be pulled to my feet. "You go clean up, and me and the girls will be waiting to make you the masterpiece that you are."

I couldn't help but shake my head and laugh at Asher's description. Asher and his companions were artists for sure. They could make someone as plain looking as me into a knock out in only a matter of minutes. I'd long since gotten used to them ignoring my personal space as they waxed and tweezed at my most sensitive bits. My scalp had gotten considerably tougher since they had started using my hair as their personal sculpture. While the end result was as fabulous as Asher had stated, the process was still a bit torturous.

While Asher went to do whatever he needed to do to get me ready, I headed to the bathroom. I'd only been in my new en-suite a few times, all of them to relieve myself. Now that I actually needed to use the other facilities, I took the time to appreciate the thoughtfulness of Patrick, my soon-to-be partner for the rest of eternity.

Not if I had anything to say about it, though.

The shower was large and, to my relief, had far fewer options to turn on than the previous one I'd had. Having so many ways to hose myself down had been overwhelming in an already crazy situation. I never wished for my simplistic plumbing back in the Glade since coming to the Core.

Even the bathtub was extravagant. Large enough to fit at least five people, it had holes all around the walls, something I hadn't had in my other bathroom. Head cocked to the side, I tried to figure out what the holes could be for, but the sound of Asher coming back with a gaggle of giggling women - his companions no doubt - reminded me I was on a time frame.

I got a big whiff of my bedclothes as I pulled them off. Nose crinkled, I made a note to myself not to wear the same clothes four days in a row. I jumped into the shower and didn't waste time trying to figure out any fancy pressure settings. I turned on the water as hot as it would go and quickly scrubbed my body and hair. The soap smelled of flowers, so intense that it made my nose itch. I'd have to find someone to ask about getting something else. While the soaps smelled pretty, I didn't want to be sneezing every minute.

"Clara? Are you done yet?" Asher's voice called through the bathroom door.

"Yes, just a moment." I scrambled out of the shower and quickly dried myself. When done, I walked out of the bathroom completely naked since I knew they would no doubt have clothes ready for me.

But when I came out, my eyes met with not four but five faces, and all the color drained from my face.

"Hello, Clarabelle."

Chapter 2

MY EYES BULGED FROM my head, and my body flushed as I realized the third person in my room was none other than Patrick himself.

His eyes skimmed over my nude form, not leering but definitely interested in what I had to offer.

I wasn't completely innocent to physical urges, but I'd never had a lover or even someone I was interested in that aspect. Not until Patrick.

My body heated at his gaze. I hated to be so vulnerable in front of him, the man, I mean monster, who kept me captive here. But at the same time, I was torn between scurrying to cover myself from embarrassment and standing there proudly just to show him he didn't bother me.

The decision was made for me when Neeka dropped a robe around my shoulders. I slipped my arms into the sleeves and tied the waist because what else was I to do? Obviously, nudity was a big deal to them, but to be like that in front of Patrick was a whole 'nother thing.

"Patrick." I nodded my head once I was fully covered. "I wasn't expecting you."

The edges of his kissable lips tipped up, his eyes full of humor and something else I couldn't place. "I can see that." He strolled toward me, and I fought the urge to step back. "Tell me, do you often occupy your rooms in such a state? If so, I must come visit more often."

My face flushed deeper, and I had a moment of wonderment. Was he flirting with me? Besides the one time we kissed which was only so he could bleed me, Patrick had been nothing but a gentleman. Well, as much as a vampire could be one. So, his unexpected flirtation caught me off guard.

Clearing my throat in an attempt to sound unaffected, I said, "No, I usually lay around in piles of cheese and pastries."

The startled expression on Patrick's face had me doing a little happy dance inside. Then Patrick did something else completely out of character. He laughed. No, not laughed, chortled. A full belly laugh that did pleasant things to my insides.

"You are something else, Clarabelle," Patrick stated and swiped a hand over his face. "It's no surprise why I chose you."

"You mean, Asher chose me," I corrected him defiantly, trying to take back some control.

His intense gaze settled on me, no longer laughing. A seriousness came over him that made me take a step back. After all, he was still the ruler of this land and a monster. Who knew what he'd do?

I expected violence from him for my insolence, but once more he surprised me. Filling up space between us, Patrick cupped my face in his hands. The feel of his skin on mine sent electric pulses through my body, and I had to admit they were not completely unwelcome.

"My cousin did, in fact, choose you, but I have made you what you are. A fact that I am quite pleased with and would hate to have to change." I could hear the threat in his voice, and the tingles inside me changed to anger.

Pushing closer to him so that our noses brushed, I forced myself to ignore the feel of his breath on my face as I snarled, "Don't forget that it is you who need me, not the other way around. I didn't ask to come here, you and Asher put me on that list. You could easily wipe me and send me back. Then you can wait another hundred years to have your chance of change."

Patrick didn't become enraged like I'd hoped. In fact, he didn't seem to be listening at all, his eyes trained on my lips. Subconsciously, I licked them and instantly regretted it. My face was so close to his that I could feel the air move between us.

A throat clearing was my only saving grace as I remembered we weren't alone. Eyes shooting to Asher, a worried look on his face, I stepped away from Patrick and took in a much-needed breath.

"Are you guys ready?" I asked, sidestepping Patrick to approach Asher and the girls. Asher gave me a disapproving look that I ignored while the girls seemed to be feeling a mixture of emotions. Fright, nervousness, and bemusement covered their faces which about summed up my own warring feelings.

"I see that you are otherwise engaged," Patrick said as if we hadn't just had a standoff in the middle of my bedroom. "I will be seeing you at dinner tonight?"

It was posed as a question, but the stern press of his lips told me it was anything but. Resisting the urge to make a rude remark, I spit out, "Sure."

Inclining his head, Patrick exchanged a look with Asher before heading for the door. When he was gone, the tension in the room lowered considerably, but they all seemed to be waiting for me to say something.

"What?" I shrugged. "He burst into my room, not the other way around."

Willow shook her head. "Honey, the whole Core is his room. You just live in it. We all do."

"So?" I cocked a hip at her. "Doesn't mean that I have to take what he gives me like I should be grateful he even looks my way. Pfft." I rolled my eyes. "I might be a prisoner, but that doesn't mean I have completely lost my spirit."

"Could have fooled me," Asher muttered, earning a glare from me. He cleared his throat once more, making me think he might be coming down with something. Could vampires get sick? He turned to his companions. "Now, I think that's quite enough drama for the day, don't you, ladies?"

The three of them eagerly nodded though I had a sneaky feeling they loved it. Why wouldn't they? If I were in their shoes, I'd have a tough time believing I wouldn't have been delighted to witness some juicy gossip about the esteemed leader, even more so about his new convert. Then again, such things were dangerous, even amongst friends.

"All right, Clara," Asher finally turned his attention back to me. "Drop the robe."

With a sigh and a shrug, I let the robe fall to the ground, my nudity no longer an issue to anyone in the room.

My mind wandered as they poked and prodded at me, sizing me up for whatever they had in store for me. Everything Asher had put me in up to this point had been lovely, but since there were no balls to go to, I couldn't imagine he had big elaborate gowns tucked away in his garment bag.

I remembered some of the outfits that the other Fold members had worn. Several of the men wore suits or some form of dress clothes. The women wore more of a variety. Some wore suits like the men, others were in dresses with slits and peek-a-boo holes so scandalous I couldn't help but hold my breath as they unzipped the bag.

The breath I held blew out in a quick whoosh. All the nerves I felt about Asher's taste felt silly. He had yet to steer me wrong; why did I think he would now?

As if reading my mind, Asher shot me a full tooth grin, exposing his sharp canines. "What? You were worried?"

"No." I scoffed and flushed. "Okay, a little. Things are different now."

"You're right. They are, and so are you." Asher nodded slightly before withdrawing the outfit completely. My first glimpse had been correct. It was a mint green pantsuit with a sheer cream-colored blouse for beneath. Though the heels of the shoes were a bit higher than I was comfortable with, I was confident the pants would make them doable.

"So, are you going to dress me all the time?" I asked as I slipped into the outfit. "Or at some point am I going to get to dress myself?"

"Well, if someone had come to their fitting appointment, you'd already have a whole wardrobe of clothes to dress in." Asher clicked his tongue at me, and I frowned.

Had I really missed that? I didn't remember anyone ever telling me about a fitting appointment. Though, they had dropped off a schedule for me every day which I had promptly ignored in favor of my bed.

The girls finished fixing my hair and makeup as I frowned. "What about my hair and makeup? Not that I need to have it done every day, I'm not used to having it done at all, but if you expect me to do it myself, you're dreaming."

Chuckling, Neeka swept a brush across my cheek. "I can come by and show you some basics to do yourself. They're easy. Won't take you more than a minute."

"And I can do your hair!" Rosel jumped in. "Not every day of course, but often enough to have some variety. I can even show you some easy tricks."

Nodding my appreciation, I let them finish off my look for that day before turning to Asher. "So, what do you think? Am I Fold worthy?"

Asher snorted. "No one is worthy in their eyes, but you'll do." He and the girls gathered up their bags and started for the door. The girls left first, leaving me alone with Asher for a moment. "I'll have them reschedule your fitting, so you'll have some clothes to wear. But you better make sure to come to it this time, or you'll be walking around the palace naked."

"Not like it bothered me before." I gave him a cheeky grin which he returned with a grandmother's disapproval.

"Be careful, Clara." Asher placed a hand on my shoulder. "Not everyone here is as forgiving as Patrick or as intrigued by you as he is. You won't be able to pull a stunt like you did today in front of the rest of the Fold without Patrick being forced to punish you."

The thought of being punished sent a shiver through me. What would it be? Whipping? The dungeons? Maybe they would just withhold food and water. I could deal with that and even the pain. There were lots of things one could endure when they put their minds to it. Then again, they were monsters. Who knew what terrors that had at their disposal?

I nodded solemnly. "I will. I promise."

"And maybe go check on your friend Marsha." Asher's suggestion caught me off guard. Why would I need to check on him? He was in the same boat as me, both destined to become one of them in every sense of the word. Fortunately for him, he was blissfully unaware of what awaited us.

More like denial.

I'd tried to tell Marsha, the butcher boy from the Inner Circle, what I had discovered, only to be called insane. He'd thrown my help back in my face, too absorbed with the lavishness his chosen had begun to cover him with. I'd been warned about that, even expected it.

The Fold wanted you to get comfortable, to feel like you were one of them, so you would easily take the change without a fuss. You would want to be like them when the time was right. So, they'd give you presents and praises, make you think you were really something special.

Not me though. Patrick hadn't even bothered to try and butter me up. Probably didn't think he needed to bother since I already knew everything about the conversion and what was in store for me. For a moment, a pang of jealousy toward Marsha filled me. I wished I could be so oblivious.

Oh, what I'd give to go back to the dark.

But I couldn't, so there was no use trying to do so. What was done was done. I had to keep moving forward and do what needed to be done to save our people. To save everyone. Even if it meant taking down the whole country to do it.

Chapter 3

I SEARCHED FOR MARSHA after that but couldn't find him. I didn't know where his rooms were. He'd been moved from the ones we had stayed in during the election as well.

Instead of spending my entire day looking for him, I decided to wait until dinner. He'd be there no doubt. I grimaced. Zara would be there as well.

Hopefully, the nasty woman would keep her distance and let me be now that I was higher up in the ranks than her. But I had little doubt that I was dreaming. If anything, she would be even more intent on belittling me and trying to take me down. She'd been vicious during the election. There was no telling what Zara would do now that she had Beaford at her back.

I ducked into the kitchens to beg some food from the cook. The older woman had been surprised to see anyone other than a servant in the kitchens, let alone a convert. So much so that she almost knocked over a whole pot of boiling soup.

"Please, what can I get for you?" she stuttered over herself, her hands going to her graying hair which had come loose from the bun she'd put it in. "If you want to sit at the dining table, I can bring you anything you want."

"Oh, no." I shook my head with a small smile, hoping to put the woman at ease. "I can make something myself if you could just point me in the right direction."

There was a gasp from the other servants in the room as well as the cook. The looks they were giving me suddenly made me feel like I'd made a faux pas. I tried to think of something to help the situation but came up empty. A heavy hand landed on my shoulder, making me jump until my eyes met that of Narq.

"Come on, Clara. Stop giving these ladies a hard time. They're just trying to do their job." Narq's casual speech to me must have been unheard of as well because all their eyes went to him. Narq brushed it off and led me to a table off to the side of the kitchen. It wasn't a bad table but definitely not what they had in the main dining hall. I decided it must be where the servants usually ate their meals.

"So, what brings you down to our neck of the woods? Tired of your life of luxury already?" He smirked at me, though I could tell he hadn't said it to be rude.

He knew as well as I did that I never wanted to be picked. Narq had even saved my life before he had been appointed to a position here in the palace. I felt like he had the better end of the deal. No pretending like you weren't a prisoner being forced to be their leader's soon-to-be bride. I bet he could even dress himself.

"Hunger actually." I smiled back, and my stomach rumbled as if to assert my point.

"What, they don't feed you over there?" he asked, laughing as he motioned toward the cook, who was watching us with a wary eye.

Ducking my head down, I chewed on my lip. "They do, but I'd been revolting."

"Revolting?" Narq asked with a raised brow. "Against food? How is that helpful to anyone?"

He sat a bowl of the steaming soup the cook had been working on in front of me. The smell of it hit my nose, and I almost growled as I shoved it into my mouth. The hot liquid hit my tongue, and I swallowed hard, my eyes watering.

"I didn't say it was a smart plan," I croaked, scooping up another spoonful but blowing on it first before putting it in my mouth. A servant girl with shy eyes and shaky hands came over and placed a basket of rolls in front of us. I thanked her which made her face turn red before digging into the buttery roll, a moan releasing from my throat.

"Well, I can't blame you really," Narq commented, watching me fill my face. "I lucked out getting this gig."

"Really? What do you do?"

Shrugging a shoulder, Narq scratched his face. "I mainly help move things around when they are setting up for events right now. Sometimes I fetch things for members of the Fold. The best part is" - he leaned in causing me to follow suit - "I get to hear all the gossip around the palace."

"Wow." I swallowed my bread and feigned interest. "That's great."

Narq rolled his eyes. "You're a horrible liar, you know that? I don't know how you made it this far."

I lifted a shoulder. "I don't know either. Just bad luck I guess."

My words caused a hard laugh from Narq. "Yeah, I could see that. Anyway, if you want to come down here and hear some of the tidbits I pick up, let me know. It might help with what you're trying to do."

I coughed as I almost choked on my spoonful of soup. A glass of water sat in front of me, and I downed it quickly. I looked up to thank the servants, but the shy girl had already taken off once more. Not letting her skittishness bother me, I turned my attention back to Narq who was glowing with glee.

"What do you mean what I'm doing?" I curled my shoulders forward and lowered my voice.

Narq placed his hands on the back of his head and leaned back in his chair. "Oh, you know the plan between you and the fearsome leader. Oh, and your guide. What's his name? Alister?"

"Asher," I corrected and then wished I hadn't. Narq knew far too much to be safe. If anyone found out what we were planning, forget wiping our memories. We'd all be dead.

"Don't worry, I won't tell anyone." Narq sat his chair back down with a thunk, causing the cook to glare at him. But one glance from me and she was dropping her gaze. What was up with that?

"Why not?" My brow raised. "I mean, you could really capitalize on this. Maybe even get converted yourself."

Narq scoffed. "Hell no. Like I'd want that. I'm happy the way I am, thank you very much. I'll leave that for you and your beefy boyfriend."

"He's not my boyfriend," I automatically answered back and then frowned. "If you don't want to tell anyone, then why tell me?"

Leaning forward, Narq had a wicked grin on his face. "Opportunity. I scratch your back ..."

"I got it." I cut him off.

I didn't know exactly what it was Narq wanted from me, or if I could give it to him when the time came. What I did know was that I was stuck in the Core until I could find an escape, my conversion was days away, and I sorely lacked in allies who believed me.

Thoughts of Marsha came to my mind, and sadness gripped my heart. He, more than anyone, needed to believe me. His insistence that I didn't know what I was talking about really rubbed me wrong. Marsha had always seemed the accepting type. Or maybe I'd just projected what kind of person I thought he was onto him. How well did I really know him?

Not well at all.

Marsha gave me meat and made chit-chat, but did that really mean we were friends? I knew at one time he had thought of us becoming more, but I'd never really entertained the thought. Now, it would be incomprehensible. There was too much going on around us, too much at stake, to worry about romance.

Fingers snapped in front of my face pulling me out of my thoughts. Shaking my head, I stared at Narq who frowned.

"I lost you there for a second. Did they do something to your head when you accepted?" He cocked his head to the side, his red hair falling over his eyes.

My lips pressed into a thin line before I answered. "No one is messing with my mind."

"Good." Narq nodded. "Then I don't have to worry about you swapping sides."

A commotion interrupted our conversation, jerking Narq and me to our feet. A rush of staff came into the kitchen, all chittering about something or another. I could only make out a few words here and there. Ones like, banquet and privileged. I had a feeling they weren't being nice about it.

"You better get going," - Narq waved his hand toward the kitchen door - "before one of your keepers finds you dirtying yourself with the rabble." There was a smile on his face, but I couldn't dismiss the bitter tone to his voice.

With one last cursory look around the kitchen, I left. Narq was right. I didn't belong in there. Not now that I belonged to them, the Crimson Fold.

I found it funny how far I'd come. Once I only knew myself as the daughter of the overseer, liked by few, feared by many. Not that I really gave them anything to fear, but that's what happened when you were the child of the boss. I'd always been the one on the outside looking in, and it seemed I'd always be there. Even now.

Outside of the Core, everyone feared and respected the Crimson Fold. Inside, most of the servants, like Narq, seemed discontent with their place, not because of the work but the people they worked for.

Not that I blamed them. I'd only met a few of the members of the Fold, and all of them, even Patrick, had a sort of carelessness about them like we were nothing more than a passing amusement.

I supposed when you lived forever that happened. Nothing had meaning anymore. How Asher had lasted this long without becoming cold and unfeeling like the others, I would never know. Perhaps it had to do with his companions, or maybe he was determined to keep whatever humanity he had left? I'd have my chance to find out if I didn't get out of here before my conversion.

Dinner wasn't too far off, and I knew based on Asher and Patrick's warning I'd have to attend. No hiding away in my room anymore. I had to play the part that was given to me, whether I wanted it or not.

I wanted to find Marsha to try and convince him once more, but by the time I found someone to direct me to his rooms, they were empty as was Tris's, Marsha's chosen partner.

Did she tell Marsha what was in store for him? Or had she been keeping him in a love-sick stupor? From what Asher said they were supposed to make us think we were their most honored guests. Celebrities. Really, it was only a way to keep us compliant until the conversion happened. Make it so we would want to change.

Pfft. Like I'd ever go quietly into anything. They'd have to take me kicking and screaming if they wanted me to become one of them.

Vampires.

Who would have thought they would exist? Certainly not me. I didn't have time for fantasies. Especially, not ones made up of horror stories. There wasn't time to be afraid of pretend monsters when things like hunger and death were so imminent in the Glade.

I see now that I had been wrong. I shouldn't have feared death. I should have feared those here in the Core. Living forever. Now that was something to be feared.

Chapter 4

NO ONE CAME TO get me for dinner, trusting I would show up on my own. I was half tempted not to go, just to prove to them I wasn't their little puppet. But I couldn't let my pride get in the way of what I needed to do.

I needed to talk to Marsha, and I knew for sure he'd be at dinner along with his partner, Tris. If tonight were anything like the others, he would be glued to the gorgeous vampire's hip, and I'd have a hard time getting him alone.

When I pushed through the doors to the dining hall, I knew I'd been right. As the smell of the bountiful feast filled my senses, my eyes locked onto one person. Marsha.

Tall and built like an ox, Marsha seemed out of place in the crowd of elites. They had tailored him suits of deep red that only proved to embellish his massiveness, especially while he stood next to Tris.

A short, plump woman, her hair had been colored since I'd seen her last. Now, it was a single shade of black with a red streak down the side. Her gown wrapped around her like a crimson glove, hugging her large hips. I wondered briefly if she had dressed them to match and then looked down at my own outfit. Would Patrick be wearing the same, so we looked like two pieces of the same puzzle? A strange part of me hoped for it, while the other sneered in disgust.

As far as the Crimson Fold were aware, I was a dutiful partner, ready and eager to become Patrick's forever. What that all included, I still wasn't sure, but I knew I didn't want any part of it.

Liar, a voice whispered in my head. *You enjoyed that kiss with him.*

That was before I knew what he was. What he planned to make me into too.

And this morning was just a fluke?

My body flushed in memory of my standoff with Patrick. It was one thing to be completely nude in front of your friends, but in front of someone you once entertained feelings for? A tingling feeling swept through me at the thought.

Patrick might be nice to look at and kind to those less fortunate, but he was still the leader of a pack of vampires and used to getting his way. My rebellion against him seemed to amuse him right now. I didn't have any fantasies that he'd let me keep going against his wishes if it caused him embarrassment.

"Clarabelle," a soft voice said from my right. Turning, I took in the sight of Violet, looking as small and beautiful as ever in a dress of soft pink. Her companion, Maleria, certainly knew how to dress someone to benefit them, unlike Tris. Then again, Violet would be pretty in anything she wore, her rosy complexion and amethyst eyes were to thank for that.

"Violet," I greeted her, a small smile on my lips. "How are you?" The question was usually used as a pleasantry, but in my case, I worried Maleria had taken advantage of Violet. She seemed so fragile that it automatically made me want to protect her.

"I'm good. Really good." She beamed back at me, and then glanced over her shoulder toward Maleria. She stood near another group of Fold members I hadn't had the pleasure of meeting. Her long blonde hair cascaded down her back and brushed the swell of her backside. Her backless white gown barely covered enough to be modest, but it had the intended effect pulling everyone's gaze to her.

Glancing back to Violet, I lowered my voice as I came closer. "Are you sure? They aren't forcing you to do anything you don't want to do?"

Violet's eyes went wide, and she shook her head as her mouth dropped open. "No," she gasped. "Maleria has been nothing but kind to me. We've even become friends."

Friends? The word caught me off guard. I mean, I shouldn't be surprised. Asher and his companions seemed to be close. They worship the ground he walks on for that matter. Then again, I've met Asher. He has a personality that was hard to hate. Maleria, though? I've never even spoken to her.

Still not convinced companions were nothing but friends, I glanced around for anyone listening in before asking, "She hasn't tried to bite you, has she?"

"Bite me?" Violet's brows furrowed. "Why would she do that?" I opened my mouth to explain, but Violet's lips curled up into a mischievous grin. "This isn't a sex thing, is it?"

"What? No," I exclaimed, shaking my head. "I just want to be sure you're okay. I don't have many friends here, and I need all the ones I have."

Giggling, Violet touched my arm. "Don't worry about me. I'm fine. What about you? How's life with the leader of all Alban?"

I didn't know how to answer her question. Did I tell her since the announcement I had only seen my soon-to-be husband once and that was this morning? I had a feeling Patrick wouldn't want everyone knowing there was discontent with his choice. It might even make those of the Fold question his authority. He couldn't handle one little girl; how was he supposed to handle the whole city?

Instead of telling her the truth, I forced a smile. "Everything is fine."

Violet's sympathetic look was not what I expected. "Don't worry. You can't expect to connect with someone right away. Besides, I'm sure he's busy running the city, you know. Just give it time." A soft smile played on her lips. "Who knows, you might just find your prince charming?"

A snort escaped before I could stop it. Prince charming? Sure, I'll add that to my list of wants.

One. Expose the Fold for the monsters they are.

Two. Get the hell out of there.

Three. Fall madly in love with the lead of the blood-sucking fiends.

Sure, that'd go over well.

"In any case," Violet continued, "it can't be worse than being sent back home, memory wiped." She paused, seemingly caught in her thoughts. After a moment, she shook her head, a sad frown on her face. "I hope Tillie is alright."

"I'm sure she is." I squeezed her hand and nodded toward Marsha, who had started this way. "Here comes Marsha."

"Hello, ladies." Marsha placed an arm around Violet and me, his warmth overwhelming me. "What are you two gossiping about over here?"

"Nothing," I quickly said.

"Clara is worried we are being taken advantage of," Violet answered right after, earning her a glare from me.

"You're still on that kick." Marsha frowned and shook his head. "Why can't you accept something for what it is? Good."

"Not everything is good," I quipped. "Some things might look good when, in fact, they are trying to kill you." I stared at him hard, trying to drill my message into him, but he didn't seem to get it.

"Too much of a good thing will kill you, sure, but this?" He waved his arm around the dining room. "How can you say this is too much? They picked us, Clara. Us, out of everyone who came. How can you be upset about that?"

"I could think of few reasons," I muttered under my breath, crossing my arms over my chest.

"Well, I'm not going to pick apart this opportunity." Marsha nudged me in the arm. "And you shouldn't either. The conversion is in a few days; you don't want to be labeled as a downer, do you?"

I started to tell Marsha how much I didn't care about what any of those monsters thought of me but thought better of it. The more I cried wolf, the more he would fight back to prove me wrong. The only way I was going to get Marsha to believe me was to show him.

Then, as if the air had been sucked out of the room, everyone quieted. I turned with the rest of them, though I knew it was Patrick. I could feel his presence as he stepped into the room. I wasn't sure why. Maybe it had to do with the blood he had taken, or maybe I was just hyper-aware of him.

You weren't this morning, that annoying voice in my head nagged.

This morning was an exception. I hadn't seen Patrick in days and hadn't expected him to show up anytime soon. For him to show up out of the blue in my room had been a surprise. A not entirely unpleasant one, but one all the same.

Thankfully, Patrick had not chosen to match his attire to mine. He wore a suit of black with a matching shirt beneath. The dark color made his already pale coloring stand out even more. His eyes scanned the room with not quite a smile on his lips. When his eyes landed on me, that hint of a grin exploded. Suddenly, I felt more naked in my three-piece suit than I did earlier this morning.

With everyone's eyes on Patrick and me, he strode across the room like he owned it. Which in a way, he did. My breath hitched against my will as if he were this all-encompassing force I couldn't understand. When he finally stood before me, I let out my breath, a sort of ease settling back over me.

Patrick took my hand in his, his lips brushing against the back of it. "Clarabelle," he murmured my name. Coming from his lips, it sounded more smooth and exotic than something you would name your cow. I hated how it made my skin prickle with goosebumps and the urge to lean toward him overwhelming.

"Patrick," I answered back, my voice breathless. The knowing expressions from Violet and Marsha snapped me out of whatever haze the vampire leader had me under. I snatched my hand back, resisting the need to rub it on my pants just to get the tingling sensation to stop.

Not bothered by my abruptness, Patrick turned his pale gaze to my friends. "Violet, how are you feeling?"

The fact that he not only remembered Violet's name but also that she had been attacked previously should have given Patrick loads of points for him. For some reason, it only irritated me more.

"I'm better now. Thank you." Violet dipped her head, a faint blush crossing her cheeks. Did Patrick have this effect on everyone or just females?

A quick glance at Marsha told me the answer. The hard look in Marsha's eyes showed he had no love for our beloved leader. The moment Patrick turned his attention to him though, his expression softened to neutral.

"I don't believe we have met yet." Patrick offered Marsha his hand. "I'm Patrick."

"I know who you are," Marsha said in a clipped voice but took Patrick's offered hand anyway. "Marsha."

"Ah, yes. You're Tris's." Patrick said it like it was an everyday occurrence to own someone.

"I'm Tris's intended yes." Marsha didn't lash out at him like I would have, simply correcting him. I wished I had his restraint.

"And how do you know my dear Clarabelle?" Patrick asked, his arm wrapping around my waist.

My body warred with me as I tried to deny the comfort in his embrace. I lost that battle as I realized I couldn't very well shove him away with so many eyes on us. We were supposed to be a loving couple, I couldn't let them think anything less, or I'd have no hope of getting away with my memory intact.

"Clara and I go way back," Marsha said. The way he used my nickname was as if he needed to prove how close he was to me.

"Is that so?" Patrick raised a brow, not at all intimidated by Marsha and his size. I guess it would be hard to be frightened when you were one of the things to be feared.

"Yes," I answered before Marsha could continue with his pissing contest. "Marsha was the butcher boy for our family."

The anger in Marsha's eyes told me I had said the wrong thing. Patrick's hand on my waist tightened, and he pulled me a bit closer to him so that I had to curl into him or else get my arm smashed.

"It is good to know my darling had someone such as you taking care of her dietary needs." Patrick smirked down at me, pinching my chin with his thumb and forefinger. "We wouldn't want just anyone handling our food."

My stomach rolled at the word. Violet and Marsha didn't react the same way I did, but then again, they didn't realize the double meaning in Patrick's words. But I did.

Food. We were nothing but food to them.

That completely contradicted the Patrick I'd met before. The one who wanted to change the system, who didn't want the humans to be treated like cattle. I hated this. I hated not knowing which Patrick I would come across. The human sympathizer or the eight-hundred-year-old vampire who saw me as nothing but a prime steak ready to be devoured.

Unable to handle the testosterone billowing around me any longer, I pushed away from Patrick and muttered an apology as I rushed for the door.

I needed air.

I had only just stepped out of the dining room doors when the last person I wanted to see came into view.

"Well, if it isn't Clarabelle." A haughty voice filled my ears, and I winced. Zara. My night couldn't get any worse.

Chapter 5

SINCE BEING CHOSEN, ZARA had stopped trying to dress to please Patrick. Her style had always been far more daring than anyone I'd ever known. Even Tris' outfit had nothing on Zara. Tonight was no different.

Her short black hair had been slicked back, her green eyes accented by vibrant red and brown makeup. It made her already striking features even more apparent. If her face didn't catch someone's attention, then her outfit would. If it could still be called an outfit.

The skin-tight red latex of her body suit covered every inch of her and still managed to be obscene. I couldn't help the blush that rose to my cheeks as I realized I could make out every curve of her body. Every curve.

Zara had always been beautiful. Not in a cute kind of way, but more like a viper that should be admired from a distance lest it strike out at you. Oh, yes, Zara was poisonous. Her action during the election proved that.

I could still remember the way that girl's face melted away. The screams were something I heard in my dreams. If it hadn't been for Narq, I would have ended the same way. Not to forget what she'd done to Violet. The fact that Zara was even here, let alone allowed to be chosen as a companion, still rubbed me raw. She had been caught in the act, and still, nothing was done.

Didn't want to cause an incident. Patrick's words still rung in my ears. It was one of the things that made me trust him less, not that I trusted him much at all now. With Zara now the companion to Beaford, a large balding man of the Fold, she was even more dangerous than before. The wicked curve of her lips said she knew it too.

I'd never hated someone before, not until Zara. She stood for everything I've ever stood against and more.

"Why so sad, pumpkin?" Zara pouted at me, patting my cheek, her long blood red nails coming too close to my eyes for comfort. "Did you have a fight with your fiancée?"

Not wanting to give her the satisfaction of knowing Patrick and I were having problems, I forced a smile on my face. "Actually, we are doing great. We spend every waking moment together."

"Is that so?" A sparkle in Zara's eyes told me she knew it wasn't. "If you two are so cozy, then why was your dear Patrick down in the feeding rooms this morning?"

"Feeding rooms?" I asked before I could catch myself.

Zara's eyes widened in surprise, her hand going to her mouth. "Oh, did I make a mistake? Has he not told you about that yet?" She clicked her tongue and snapped her fingers. "Well, shoot. I guess the cat's out of the bag now." The delight on her face contradicted her words.

"What are the feeding rooms?" As she had said the cat was out of the bag, I might as well find out whatever I could.

Zara examined her nails as if she were bored with our conversation already. "Exactly what they're called." My brow furrowed at her words which made her sigh impatiently. "They're for Fold members who don't have a companion." She paused a sly smile on her lips. "You know, to feed on."

She played with the collar of her outfit and then slid it down for me to see the two puncture wounds on her neck. "Beaford never goes down. He says my blood is all that he needs." She gave a girlish sigh.

My nose crinkled up in disgust. The thought of that disgusting excuse for a man sinking anything into me made my stomach want to revolt.

"Oh, don't act like such a prude." Zara snapped. "Your boy, Marsha, is probably getting his rocks off just as well with Tris. She can be quite the lover, I hear." Zara obscenely licked her lips.

For some reason, the notion of Marsha and Tris together in more of a friendly way upset me. Which it shouldn't since we didn't have a relationship. I'd just decided before we weren't really even friends. But wasn't it he who not too long ago asked me to consider dating him? Then he turns around and gets with Tris?

"Oh, my," Zara placed her hand on her chest with a giggle. "You don't like Marsha, do you? Does Patrick know he has competition?"

I shook my head quickly. "Marsha and I are just friends."

"Sure, you are," Zara smirked, placing her hand on my shoulder. "Don't worry, I won't tell your little secret. It's safe with me." She winked at me, and I had the sudden urge to knock her lights out.

"There's no secret. So, nothing to tell."

"If you say so." Zara shrugged. "But if you don't want people to start asking questions," - she leaned forward, her voice lowering - "and I mean Fold member kind of people, then you better start playing your part because I'm not the only one who's noticed Patrick's presence in the feeding rooms."

With that, Zara brushed past me and into the dining hall behind me. The sound from the hall filled my ears, and I knew I had to go back. If not for appearance's sake, then to ask Patrick about what Zara had told me.

Smoothing my hands over my jacket, I took a deep breath in and let it out. Back to the horde.

When I stepped into the dining room, everyone had already sat down for dinner. My seat on the right side of Patrick was the only one empty. As I made my way to my chair, it felt as if all eyes were on me - which they probably were.

I was the only one acting out of the norm. I should be like Marsha or Violet, half in love with my partner. Sadly, I might be too stubborn to ever fall in love, let alone with someone who I didn't trust as far as I could throw him.

My eyes met Marsha's as I passed by him and Tris. I nodded at the question in his eyes, the one that asked if I was alright. For someone so invested in their partner, like Zara claimed, he paid more attention to me than he should. I hated to admit a part of me reveled in it.

"Clarabelle, how happy to have you back," Patrick's smooth as butter voice announced my arrival as I stepped up to my chair. Patrick stood and pulled my chair out before I could do it myself. Locking eyes with him, he raised a brow. Would I really make a big deal about him acting like a gentleman? The childish side of me wanted to let out a snide remark, but since I was supposed to be playing nice tonight, I let it slide. Besides, there was a whole dinner to show my rebellion.

"Thanks," I muttered, sitting down with as much grace as I could muster - which in all honesty wasn't much.

I stared down at the bowl in front of me. The same stew I'd eaten around lunchtime stared back at me, it's savory scent tickling my nose. There were even rolls placed on their own little individual plates with several types of butter.

In the Glade, people were starving, and here they must have more than one option for a spread. The sheer waste made me hate the Fold just a little more.

"Clarabelle?"

I jerked my eyes away from the butter to meet Patrick's questioning gaze. "Yes?"

"I asked if your meal was unsatisfying?" His lips turned down into a frown.

Brow furrowed, I shook my head. "No, it's fine."

"Well, you were glaring at it like you wanted to stab it," Beaford chuckled, and for the first time, I noticed how close he and Zara were seated to us.

Forcing my face into what I hoped was a neutral expression, I said flatly, "The poultry hasn't done anything to me to deserve such treatment. Though I could think of a few who have."

To my satisfaction, Beaford's grin fell, and a scowl sat in its place. If no one else noticed my threat, at least he did. Zara glowered at me from Beaford's side but didn't say anything. I doubt they wanted everyone to know they had conspired together to get rid of me. They probably still were.

Zara was the type to want to be on top. It was probably eating her alive for me to be at Patrick's right where she thought she should be.

Beaford, on the other hand, seemed like the type to want to play puppet master. He'd probably love nothing more than to see Zara where I sit. He'd have a hold over her for the rest of her life, which would be eternal if she converted.

The pair of them together was something to worry about. I'd just have to add them to the list of things to watch out for. On it already was the rest of the Fold members as well as a lot of the staff. Even Asher had a place on my list, though it was nearer to the bottom than the two across from me.

"I heard you like to spend your time in the kitchen," Zara said, a nasty gleam in her eyes. "Why ever would you want to go there?"

Not taking her bait, I shrugged. "I was hungry. Plus, I got to pretest this delicious soup." I dipped my spoon into the bowl and brought it up to my mouth. As I swallowed, a hum of pleasure crossed my lips as my eyes closed. It was as good as it was the first time.

"With that kind of reaction, I must ask what are we waiting for?" The laughter in

Patrick's voice caused me to look in his direction. His eyes were focused on me, his lips curved up in amusement. There was an underlying heat to his gaze that caused me to blush.

"Oh, Patrick. Look at the dear." Tris giggled beside Marsha, flashing her sharpened canines. "She's positively precious. I can see why you wanted her for yourself."

"Yes, she must be quite the plaything." This came from another member, whose name I didn't know yet. Male with a bald head and hungry look in his eyes. I shifted in my seat uncomfortably.

"Marcus," Patrick warned. "That is my future wife you speak of."

"Oh, now you've done it." Tris giggled again. The sound of it made me want to throw a knife at her. Maybe it'd hit her in the heart. Did the stake have to be wood? Mental note: look up ways to kill vampires.

The others laughed with her, enjoying my discomfort and Patrick's ire. There was one thing I liked less than being center of attention, and that's being the butt of a joke.

"I'm no one's plaything." The growl in my voice caused the laughter to die.

"The kitten has claws. I like that." Marcus licked his lips, not even scared of Patrick's warning. I knew then that if it came down to it, Marcus would be the first to die. I didn't want to be at that man's mercy ever.

"Clara is from the Glade," Marsha said, interrupting their laughter. "They're more sheltered there. I suspect she doesn't even know what you are talking about."

Tris placed a hand on Marsha's, pouting up at him and then turned her pouty gaze on me. Just seeing her hand on him made my blood boil. "You poor dear. It must have been dreadful for you there."

"Best place I've ever lived." I gave her a toothy grin which probably looked more like a snarl. Patrick's cool hand found my leg beneath the table and squeezed until I winced.

"Now, now. No more poking fun at my fiancé." Patrick's voice was playful but had a threat to it that had the rest of the members settling back in their chairs.

While the table resumed their meals, I put my hand on top of Patrick's, my nails digging into his hand until I drew blood. Patrick sucked in a sharp breath but didn't release me.

Glaring at him, I hissed lowly, "We need to talk."

Nodding slightly, Patrick said, "That we do."

Chapter 6

I PACED BACK AND forth in the library, waiting for Patrick to show. We hadn't had a chance to talk alone at dinner, and I'd only barely been able to sneak in my love for reading into the conversation. I just hoped he caught the hint.

After thirty minutes and Patrick still a no-show, I busied myself looking for anything and everything on vampires. Might as well get something out of the trip.

The shelves were filled with books about so many topics. From cooking to ancient Egypt, whatever that was. I feared I wouldn't find anything else like the guide I'd found the first time until I neared the mythology section.

Here there were books on all kinds of creatures. Werewolves. Fairies. Ghosts.

Even vampires. I tried not to think about the likelihood that other creatures existed and started pulling books off the shelves. My first and foremost concern was vampires, all the rest could wait their turn.

With a pile of books next to me, I sat at one of the back tables my nose buried in a book about someone called Vlad. He had been rumored to be a vampire, drinking the blood of his enemies and impaling their heads on spikes to warn others. Whether he actually was a vampire had never been confirmed, but even if he wasn't, he was someone to be feared.

"You're not going to find anything useful in there."

I jumped to my feet my hand going for a paperweight sitting on the table. When my eyes focused in on Patrick, I relaxed but didn't drop the paperweight. You never know.

"I wasn't sure you would come," I admitted, leaning against the side of the table while keeping my eyes on him. He might be on my side - supposedly - but he was still a threat.

"How could I miss your not so subtle hint?" Patrick grinned, his fangs peeking out for me to see.

"I thought I was pretty subtle," I grumbled, fiddling with a book on the table.

"Well, you already declared quite venomously how much you hate reading, anyone would find it peculiar for you to go to a library. Unless it was for a secret rendezvous."

I flushed at the implications in his words. I remembered when he was talking about. Who wouldn't? It was probably recorded somewhere I could watch my embarrassment over and over again.

Saving me from my humiliation, Patrick's eyes flickered down to my hand where I gripped the large glass weight tightly. "Plan to do something with that?"

I shrugged. "Possibly. Depends on how our talk goes."

He threw his head back and laughed, a sound that tingled along my skin, making me warm all over. I wished he'd stop doing that. Gaze locked on me, Patrick came toward me slowly as if I were a deer that was going to spook at any second. "You must not have very high hopes for this meeting then."

"I like to keep my expectations low."

"I see that." Patrick didn't stop in front of me but moved past to sit in the chair I'd been in. He picked up the book I'd been reading before setting it aside with a frown. He did this to four more books before I finally spoke up.

"Can I help you?"

He set another book to the side, and then leaned back in the chair, propping his feet up on the table. "None of these" - he gestured with his hand at the books - "are going to tell you what you want to know."

"And you are?"

"Within reason."

The way he said it made me think he wouldn't tell me anything that wouldn't benefit him from me knowing. What Zara had said came back to my mind, and suddenly I wanted nothing more than to know about the feeding.

Placing the paperweight down on the table, I turned back to him with my arms crossed. "Okay. What are the feeding rooms?"

The moment I asked the question, Patrick's face darkened. "Who told you about those?"

"Why does it matter?" I countered. "If we're supposed to be partners, not just in public but working toward our cause, then I need to know everything. Not just the bits and pieces you deem me worthy to know."

Patrick's brow furrowed, and he seemed to think on my words. Finally, after I thought he might dismiss me altogether, he nodded. "Very well. You're right. We are partners. In public and behind closed doors." He shifted in his seat, the first time he ever showed me discomfort. "There are parts of being my chosen one that I have kept from you. Things I didn't think you would be inclined to do."

My mouth went dry, and I swallowed thickly. "You mean letting you feed on me."

Nodding, Patrick dropped his eyes to his lap. "If we were really lovers, it would be second nature. Something that wouldn't even be in question, but since we are barely confidants," - he flashed me a wry grin - "I thought it best to get my nourishment elsewhere."

"But won't that get you in trouble?" I huffed. "Or I mean, draw attention to us?"

"Yes, it will. Eventually." Patrick drew out that last word and then shook his head. "They already think you are an innocent, so it won't be too hard to play off that you are shy about being so intimate."

"No," I quickly snapped. The thought of the Fold thinking I was any more innocent than they already did irritated me. I needed them to see me as a force to be reckoned

66

with, not some little lamb being brought to slaughter. At Patrick's surprised expression, I added, "I mean, if we don't at least pretend that part, it'll be hard to make them believe I'm a willing convert."

"You want me to bite you?" The uncertainty in his question made him seem more vulnerable in that moment like he wasn't some all-powerful vampire who had my life in the palm of his hand.

I struggled to answer, not wanting to hurt his feelings. "Well, not really. I wouldn't willingly subject myself to pain if I didn't have to, but if you just did it the once, enough to show a mark, then maybe it would help our cause."

Patrick smirked at me as if he were trying not to laugh. "Subject yourself to pain, is it?"

"Well, yeah? I mean, I have to get shots because they are required, but I wouldn't do it because I wanted to. Though, I might want to have some wine first, if it will hurt too much."

Now, Patrick was really laughing. Completely confused at his reaction, I moved a bit away from him. Had he lost his mind?

"I apologize," Patrick said after a moment, brushing his hair out of his face.

"Your innocence is far more amusing than I thought."

"My innocence?" I quirked a brow. "You've lost me."

He gestured for me to come closer, and against my better judgment, I did. Stopping just in front of him, I waited for his explanation.

"What you felt the night of the election was a nick. Not a true feeding. It only hurt because I did not truly bite you." Patrick's eyes slid down from my face and settled on my neck. I took a hesitant step back as he reached for me. He stopped and met my eyes. "You have to trust me, Clara. On this, I promise you, I have not lied."

My curiosity overriding my better judgment, I stepped toward him once more. His hands slid beneath my hair to cradle my head. Rising from the chair, his breath brushed against my neck. My heart beat at a rapid pace as the anticipation for pain heightened.

Hands sweating, I didn't know what to do with them. Did I put them in my lap? Was I supposed to hold on to him? Patrick's semi-kiss was the closest I'd ever been to a male, so it seemed only normal to freak out.

"Relax," Patrick murmured in my ear, his lips brushing the curve of it. Him telling me to relax made it even harder to do. My body was telling me to jerk my leg up and hit him where it hurt, while the other part of me wanted to see what all the fuss was about.

Smooth lips caressed the side of my neck, where my pulse throbbed like a beating drum. My breathing came in faster as I tried to decide if I was really crazy enough to let him bite me.

I'd spent too long in my head fighting over it because the sting of his fangs piercing my skin startled me. I jumped in place, but Patrick's arm wrapped around my waist, pulling me toward him. Probably a good idea or I'd have ripped a sizable chunk out of myself.

Patrick's bite was nothing like when he nipped me at the election. Sure, there was a small sting where he bit me, but then as he started sucking, taking my essence into himself, a kind of euphoria filled my senses.

My head seemed as light as a cloud as my eyes fluttered closed. It was as if I could hear my own heart pumping my blood through my veins, more than happy to offer itself to the vampire holding me. Along with the feeling of floating came something else. Something strange and new to me.

Desire.

My very being filled with it, my hands roaming for something to grab hold of and finding their way into Patrick's shirt. I held on for dear life as my breathing became gasps. The sensations were overwhelming, and I wanted, no, needed more.

One of my hands slid upward, pressed on the back of Patrick's head, keeping him against my neck. Afraid he would stop and take away this feeling. A feeling I'd never thought I would feel or ever want.

Patrick wrapped my legs around his waist, holding me close to him. He seemed as consumed as I did. Part of me wondered how it felt for him, but with the hot need monopolizing my every thought, I didn't have time to care.

Suddenly, Patrick was ripped away from me and with him the addicting feeling. My eyes snapped open searching for Patrick, a voice spoke, but I couldn't hear it over the panic ringing in my head. I wanted it back. I needed it.

Eyes wild, I found Patrick several feet away pressed against the bookshelf. His mouth stained red with my blood. The look in his eyes - the hunger - had to be the same as my own.

Hands shook me, the same voice saying my name. Who else was here? Who stopped us? If Patrick stood over there, then ...

My head cleared slowly as the person in front of me came into focus. Large shoulders, brown hair, and a look of concern in kind eyes.

Marsha.

"What?" I asked, and even to me, my voice sounded off. Like I was miles away and not sitting right there in the library.

"Are you okay?" Marsha asked, his hand going to my neck before shouting over his shoulder. "What the hell did you do to her?"

Patrick licked his lips and chuckled. "Nothing you haven't already had done to yourself."

Marsha's eyes widened, and then they came back to my face. "This. This was what you were talking about?"

"Oh, so now you believe me." I giggled, a drunken feeling overtaking me.

"I'm sorry, Clara. I didn't understand what you meant." Marsha shook his head. "I thought it was just some strange kink Tris had. I honestly didn't think it was ..." His words trailed off, his eyes sliding back to Patrick. "Vampires."

Clapping filled my ears. Patrick straightened from the wall, his hands coming together making the booming sound. "Congratulations, Marsha. You've finally figured it out. Though, I'm sure my girl has been trying to tell you all along."

"She's not your girl," Marsha snarled, standing in front of me and cutting off my view of Patrick.

Patrick stopped in front of him, but I could only see his side. Marsha was too tall. I pushed at his side, urging him to move, but it was like moving an ox.

"Hey," I yelled, pointing at Marsha's shoulder. "I'm in charge here not you."

"You heard the lady. Move aside," Patrick commanded.

"No," Marsha crossed his arms over his chest, his muscles bulging beneath this shirt. "You aren't getting near her. We're leaving."

Patrick let out an aggravated sigh. "The only thing you are doing is killing her. If you don't let me heal her, she's going to bleed out."

At Patrick's words, my hand went to my neck. Warm wetness came away, and when I looked at my hand, it was covered in blood. The same blood on Patrick's lips.

Marsha glanced back at me, an internal fight clear on his face. I nodded to let him know I was okay. If he didn't let Patrick heal me, then we had to at least stop the bleeding.

"He hasn't killed me so far." I offered him a small smile which wasn't returned. Sighing, I added, "He needs me. He can't kill me yet. Besides, no one wants Zara to take my place more than me."

Frowning but moving out of the way, Marsha grabbed Patrick's arm as he came by. "Hurt her, and it will be the last thing you do."

Patrick pulled his arm away from him, not even acknowledging his threat. I let my legs fall apart to allow him to step between them, more trusting now for some reason. His hand cupped the back of my neck, but this time, he simply lowered his head to my neck.

I expected him to bite me again, so when a quick lapping of his tongue took the place of pain, I flushed. It shouldn't have been erotic. Someone was licking my neck, there was nothing attractive about that. But somehow it was. When Patrick moved away from my neck, the heat in his eyes had returned. I wasn't the only one who had been affected.

"Alright, buddy. You healed her. Now, it's time for bed." Marsha tried to shove between us, but Patrick wouldn't move.

His eyes stayed locked on mine as he said, "She is my responsibility. I will see her to her rooms."

"Yeah, right," Marsha scoffed. "So you can take advantage of her some more? I don't think so. I'll see her to bed, and then tomorrow we are leaving."

"Lady's choice," Patrick murmured, his hand stroking mine, making it hard to think.

Swallowing, I licked my lips. "I think it's probably better if Marsha took me."

I could tell that wasn't the answer Patrick wanted to hear, but he nodded. Stepping back from me, he let Marsha take his place.

Standing from the table, my legs threatened to give out. Marsha wrapped an arm around my waist, holding me against his side. "I've got you."

My eyes never left Patrick's as Marsha led me away from him and toward the door. It wasn't until a bookshelf got in the way did our gaze break. Instantly, I missed it.

I wanted to go back. To talk to Patrick. To just be near him. My blood begged me to return, and I knew that's why I couldn't.

Space. I needed space. I wasn't sure what I expected to happen when Patrick fed on me, but it certainly wasn't this desire to

be close to him. Now, my head was all sorts
of mixed up. What did it mean?

75

Chapter 7

I MADE MARSHA DROP me off at my rooms. I didn't want the servants to gossip about him being in them this late. The last thing we needed was for Zara to have even more ammunition to get rid of me.

Since when did I not want to leave? The thought came so suddenly, I sat up in bed.

Did Patrick have such a hold on me now that the very thought of leaving him pained me? No. I could leave if I wanted to, but part of me wouldn't like it. The part that still begged me to go back to the library or, worse yet, find Patrick in his rooms.

The image of finding Patrick in his bed made a shudder race through me. This overwhelming need to be near him had to stop, but even as I thought it, my need to go to him grew.

Stubbornness filled me, and I wrapped my arms around my pillow. Rocking back and forth, I clenched my teeth demanding the feeling to go away. *I'm strong. I don't need him. He's a vampire. A monster.*

Was he really? a traitorous voice whispered. *He didn't seem much like a monster when he was feeding on you.*

That's the reason exactly! He had to feed on me. That's not normal.

You liked it. Admit it.

Snarling, I gripped the pillow harder, refusing to admit it. Sure, when I was still in the cloud of desire, I'd wanted nothing more than to continue where we left off, but now I knew it was a bad idea. The whole thing should have never happened.

A knock on my door jerked me out of my thoughts. Not strong enough to get up and answer the door, I asked, "Who is it?"

There was a pause before a familiar voice said, "Asher. Can I come in?"

I chewed on my lower lip, not sure if I should see him while I was like this. I was a hop skip and a jump away from darting out of my room in search of Patrick. That wasn't something I wanted Asher to see.

Maybe he knows how to stop it?

That thought alone had me granting him entry.

The door creaked open, and Asher's eyes scanned the darkened room until they landed on me in the bed. His silhouette came toward me, and I couldn't look at him as he turned on the lamp on the nightstand.

The bed dipped, and Asher's hand touched mine. I flinched, still not meeting his gaze.

"Patrick told me what happened," were his first words.

I didn't answer him and just kept staring at the duvet, my eyes tracing the lines of the pattern in it.

"How are you feeling?" Asher tried again.

"Okay," I croaked and then cleared my throat. "I'm fine."

"You don't look fine." Asher brushed my hair back behind my ear, his fingers going to trace the spot where Patrick had bitten me. There were marks there, I had made sure to look, but the two pen pricks had stopped bleeding.

"I don't know what to say." I slowly lifted my head to meet his concerned eyes. "I let him bite me."

"Yes, you did." Asher nodded and then moved closer, taking my hands in his. "Now, instead of beating yourself up about it, how about telling me how it made you feel?"

"Dirty," I immediately answered.

Asher gave me an impatient look.

"And ... good. It felt good. Really good. My body was on fire, and nothing else mattered." It was like once I started talking about it, I couldn't stop. "If Marsha hadn't stepped in, I don't know if I would have stopped him." I gripped Asher's hand, my eyes wide as panic filled me. "I could have died!"

Asher clicked his tongue. "I highly doubt that. Patrick is one of the oldest of us. He has better control than most. He wouldn't have drained you."

"How do you know?"

"We need you still, of course."

"Of course." Sarcasm dripped from my words.

"Also, Patrick cares for you. He would never hurt you if he could help it." Asher shook his head. "Your friend showing up wouldn't have mattered."

"But why do I feel like this?" I removed my hands from his and grabbed at the front of my shirt. "I can't stop thinking about Patrick, and it's taking all I have just to stay in this bed and not run to him."

Asher chuckled. "It's normal. Especially for first-timers. It'll go away by morning. I promise."

I nodded but wasn't entirely convinced.

"Until then." Asher stood and went to the bathroom. The light clicked on, and then there was the sound of water running. Asher came back into the room with a glass of water. "You need to drink plenty of water and ..." He dug around in his pocket and withdrew two pills. "Take these. If things got out of hand like you said, you need to replenish your blood supply. These will help."

I took the pills from him and downed them with the water. Once I started drinking, I found myself parched and drained the glass. Asher took it from me and refilled it, sitting it on the nightstand.

"Better?"

"Much."

It was true. After drinking the water, I felt much more like myself. The urge to go to Patrick was still there but not as strong as before. I probably could even go to sleep now.

"Do you want to talk some more about it?" Asher asked, not looking like he would be leaving anytime soon.

"No." I shook my head. "I'm good now. I think. Just need a good night's sleep."

"Not even about leaving?" Asher raised his brow, and I ducked my head guiltily.

"That was Marsha, not me," I muttered, only half lying. I'd planned on leaving as soon as I could without getting caught, but I hadn't shared that with anyone. Marsha only wanted me to leave because of Patrick. If I weren't getting all cozy with him, he wouldn't have even thought anything different.

Which reminded me that I'd have to talk to him tomorrow. Now that he knew what was going on, he'd start acting differently. Would he still let Tris bite him? Hopefully, he was smart enough to not give away that anything had changed, but I wasn't so sure.

"Clara?" Asher said. "What is it?"

"Just worried Marsha will do something stupid," I admitted and then let out a harsh laugh. "He didn't believe me when he had blood on his own neck but seeing me with Patrick ..." I laughed again, palming my face. "You should have seen them, Asher. Acting like a bunch of dogs trying to see who could piss on me first."

Asher smiled. "Well, when you have two alphas vying for your attention, it stands to reason there will be bloodshed."

I winced at the mention of blood and hoped it wasn't mine being shed. "Still, Marsha shouldn't have needed me to be the one in danger to convince him. He should have listened to me." I slammed my fist on the bed, but the padding kept it from making any sound. "I'm not the one who needs protecting. He does."

Asher chuckled. "No one sees you as a damsel in distress." I shot him a look. "Okay, everybody but myself and Patrick does, but that's what you need to change." Asher stood. "You've hidden away too long. Stayed to yourself. You need to get out there and show them you are a queen - which you will be once you are at Patrick's side."

"And when will that be? Before or after the conversion?" I wrinkled my nose at him.

"Before." When Asher saw the distaste on my face, he waved a finger at me. "Now, none of that. We don't plan on you going through with the conversion, but if you don't marry Patrick, then you won't have any power. You barely have any now."

"But the conversion is only a few days away. How are we going to get married in that small amount of time?" I asked, not seeing how this would work.

"Leave that to me." Asher placed a hand on his chest with a grin. "You can't be converted until you are married, and you can't get married without a huge party to celebrate, right?"

My brow furrowed. "Uh, right?"

"And huge parties take time to plan. Especially, when it's the leader of all of Alban's. Everyone who is anyone will want to be there, and the whole event needs to be televised to the whole ring." The more Asher talked, the more worried I became.

While delaying the conversion sounded like my best bet for finding a way out of here, getting married wasn't. I hadn't ever thought I'd marry anyone, let alone someone I barely knew. Plus, once Patrick and I were married, I'd have even less time to myself, taking away any chances of getting away and warning the people.

"So, what do you say?" Asher asked.

I stared at him. I hadn't heard a thing he'd said. I nodded, hoping it would be enough to make him think I'd been listening. I just hoped I wasn't agreeing to sacrifice my firstborn.

Asher clapped his hands together in delight, beaming down at me. "Great. I'll let

Patrick know and have all the preparations started. The girls are going to flip. This is going to be the biggest party I've ever planned." He tapped his chin in thought. "I'll definitely need Daphne for this. I don't see how I could handle it all on my own. There is so much to do with so little time!"

Leaving my bedside with more of a skip in his step, Asher stopped at my door. Turning back to me, he said, "Tomorrow, you need to find that friend of yours and get him on board. We can't have him ruining everything because he's jealous."

"Okay," I answered because I didn't see how I could tell him no.

"And drink water." He pointed at the cup of water with a stern look. Then he was gone, and I was alone in my room again.

Collapsing back on the bed, I wondered what the heck I'd gotten myself into. I was supposed to be finding a way to get away from Patrick and the Fold, not get more involved. Now, not only did I need to start putting my foot down, but I had to have this elaborate wedding that I didn't even want.

Closing my eyes, I let my mind wander back to when life was simpler, when I was only the overseer's daughter and the most I had to worry about was making friends. Now, making friends was the furthest thing

from my mind. Making enemies was far
more worrying.

85

Chapter 8

ASHER HAD BEEN RIGHT. When I woke the next morning, the urge to be near Patrick had lessened. I still felt it, but it was more of an annoying itch in the back of my mind. That, I could handle.

I chugged the water on my nightstand and stood from the bed. I sat back down as the world started to spin. Waiting for the lightheadedness to stop, I breathed in through the nose and out through my mouth.

When I felt like I could chance standing again, I slowly inched to my feet. The world didn't spin on its axis this time, and I took a few hesitant steps toward the bathroom. Reaching the sink, I realized the only cup I had was back by my bed.

Glancing longingly back at the cup, I knew I wouldn't make it back there without laying back down. Screw it. I used my hands to cup up the water from the sink and drank until I felt sick.

Note to self: don't ignore advice from vampires. They mean business.

My nightgown stuck to my skin from where I had sweat through the night. Dragging it over my head, I stepped into the shower. My skin felt hot like I had a fever. I turned the shower on to the lowest setting I could handle and let the cool water wash over my heated skin.

If I'd known there'd be so many side effects from giving blood, I wouldn't have let Patrick bite me. Did Marsha get the same kind of symptoms? Did he just brush them off as him being sick or hungover? How had he really been so blind until now?

My mind raced with all the possibilities of why Marsha couldn't see what I was telling him was true until last night.

Cause he likes you.

If he liked me, he wouldn't have been so quick to dismiss me or my warnings. He'd have believed me the first time, and he sure as heck wouldn't have been necking with Tris.

Anger getting the better of me, I washed my hair aggressively, almost yanking the hair from my head. Rinsing off quickly, I could no longer wait to see Marsha and give him a piece of my mind. I wasn't someone he could just like when it was convenient for him. He either liked me or didn't.

What about you and Patrick?

What about it? I was in the same situation as Marsha, but at least I wasn't just rolling over and accepting Patrick as my partner. Sure, I was attracted to him. He had a certain kind of allure about him that would attract anyone. But I hadn't let him bite me until last night, and even that was only because Zara had put the thought in my head.

Liar.

Okay, so it wasn't all Zara. Morbid curiosity and self-interest. Maybe more curiosity than anything but still, I'd done it, and I'm fine. I wasn't mooning after him. At least, not anymore. I still thought he could be a jerk and wasn't telling me everything, something I hoped to remedy soon.

Getting out of the shower, I dried off so fast I had towel burn before shoving on the first clothes I found, which happened to be some dress thing of air peachy material. Must have been accidentally put in my closet. I didn't have the time or the energy to find something else to wear. I found a pair of strappy sandals that Asher would praise me for wearing before heading for the door. I hadn't bothered to put on makeup or dry my hair - which I realized when I started getting odd looks in the hallway.

Determined not to let them bother me, I straightened my back and stomped toward Marsha's rooms. I was on a mission, and judgmental vampires and servants weren't part of that mission. Banging on Marsha's door, I waited impatiently tapping my foot. "Marsha. Open up. I know you're in there."

"Do you?"

I spun around to see the owner of the voice leaning against the hallway wall. "Narq, what are you doing over here?"

"I could ask you the same thing, but I can clearly see you are looking for our boy Marsha." Narq gestured to the door I'd been pounding in to. "But I'm sad to announce he's not here."

"He's not?" I glanced at the door and back to him. "Where did he go?"

Narq smirked. "Where most people go first thing in the morning." When I only stared in confusion, he leaned forward and whispered, "Breakfast."

The mention of food made my stomach rumble, reminding me I hadn't fed it today. That, of course, caused me to think of feeding Patrick which led me right back to Marsha. It seemed I was in a never-ending cycle that would only end with someone dead.

"Need me to show you the way?" Narq offered me his arm which I brushed by on my way down the hall. "I'll take that as a no, but I'll keep you company in any case."

"If you must."

We walked in silence for a few moments, my determined footsteps causing my shoes to make loud clacking noises on the floor. Narq kept up with me well enough but seeing as he had over a foot of height on me, I didn't expect anything less. This was probably a light stroll to him, rather than the death march it was for me.

"You must really need to talk to Marsha. Did something happen? Have a lover's quarrel?" Narq asked.

I glanced over at him and saw the smirk on his lips. "Why does everyone think Marsha and I are dating?" I growled, my feet stomping even harder on the tile. "We're just friends. That's it."

"Could have fooled me." Narq chuckled. "Plus, the way he looks at you when he thinks you can't see him says it all."

"He looks at me?"

"Oh yeah," Narq nodded. "Like a lovesick pup. Pretty disgusting if I'm being honest."

"Well, he sure has a crappy way of showing it." I sniffed. "Until last night that is. Now, I'm afraid he might do something stupid."

"Last night?" Narq asked, raising a brow. "What happened last night?"

I sighed. "Nothing. He caught me with Patrick and went all alpha male on him. Trying to tell Patrick I don't belong to him. Now, I just need to find him and make sure he doesn't do something that'll get us both killed."

Narq whistled. "Man, the drama of the elite. Can't say I envy you."

"I'm not elite." I shot him a glare. "I'm the same as you. Less than that if you go by what Zara says. I'm from the Glade —"

"Which makes you no less than me," Narq interrupted. "But you have to accept that you are above the rest of us. You are going to be treated differently from now on. By everyone. Your friends. Your family even, if you ever get to see them again."

"Yeah, the likelihood of that happening is looking pretty slim." Sadness came over me at never seeing my father again. My stepfamily, well, there was no love lost there. Julianna had been nasty to me from the moment I stepped into her home. Lea, while not as bad as her older sister, still didn't treat me as equals. Their mother was even worse, though she was subtler about it.

"I'm getting married," I said all of a sudden, my footsteps slowing. "To Patrick."

"Well, that's no surprise." Narq nodded. "It would make sense for you to get married to him before you are brought into the Fold."

"It's going to be this big spectacle no doubt, with cameras and big puffy dresses. It's supposed to be the happiest day of my life, and all I can think about is whether or not my father will be able to walk me down the aisle." My eyes welled up, and I turned my back on Narq so he wouldn't see me cry.

His hand landed on my shoulder, not turning me around but patting me with an awkward sort of rhythm. "It's alright. I'm sure if you asked Patrick, he might make an exception. Wouldn't do for the public to see their soon-to-be first lady unhappy."

"Queen," I quipped. "I'd rather be a Queen than the first lady. Then at least, I could sound like I had some kind of power."

"Sure, you will." Narq grinned at me as I turned around. "You'll be kissing babies and saving orphanages in no time, all in the guise of starting a revolution that is." Narq winked at me as he gestured toward the dining room door. "Looks like this is where I leave you."

I hadn't even realized we were so close when I'd stopped. I'd been so caught up in my thoughts that my feet moved on their own. At least, I knew I could go into automatic mode if need be. I had a feeling I would need it more and more in the days to come.

"Thanks, Narq," I said before realizing he'd already left. Shrugging, I headed into the dining room. Might as well get something to eat before I yelled at Marsha.

Unfortunately, the moment I stepped into the dining room, I was confronted by a horde of female companions and Fold members alike.

"Is it true?" Violet asked.

Someone else I didn't recognize pushed in front of Violet. "Are you really getting married?"

I couldn't get a word out as they all started to ask their questions in rapid concession. All of them about my and Patrick's wedding. Asher had been busy, it seemed.

Searching over the heads of my questioners, I saw Patrick coming toward me. Our eyes met, and for a brief moment, I couldn't breathe. No one else in the room mattered but him. My blood pulsated in response to his presence, and my heartbeat quickened as his pushed through the crowd to take me by the elbow.

"Now, that's enough questions for today. Let Clarabelle get some food in her stomach before you get into the heavy ones." Patrick smiled that melting smile that had all the women parting to let us by.

With my arm firmly looped through Patrick's, we made our way to the breakfast table. He leaned down when everyone else was taking their seats and asked, "How are you feeling?"

I glanced up at him and then quickly back down as my face heated up. I thought this crap was supposed to be gone already! "I'm fine." I quickly snapped and then realized how I sounded. "I mean, I'm good. Asher came by and gave me some pills and ..."

"That's good." Patrick cut me off, saving me from my word explosion. "I'm glad you are feeling better. As you see," - he gestured with his head toward the still chittering women - "Asher has already started working on our nuptials. How do you feel about that?"

I stared at him.

Laughing, Patrick patted my hand as we sat down. "Don't worry, it won't be all that bad. I'm sure we can keep it to less than a thousand guests."

"That's reassuring," I said dryly.

I had just taken a drink of my orange juice when Patrick said, "Of course, we'll need to make sure your family comes as well."

I choked on the liquid, some of it going up my nose, causing a burning sensation. Coughing, I grabbed my napkin. Patrick watched me with growing amusement when he should have looked concerned.

"What?" I coughed once more. "What did you say?"

"Your family," Patrick repeated. "You will want them here, won't you?"

Nodding my head so quickly I feared it might fall off, I said, "Yes, yes. I just didn't think outsiders were allowed to these kinds of things."

Patrick shrugged. "Not usually but this is a special exception. Plus, who's going to walk you down the aisle?"

Well, I'll be. I'd come here to ask Patrick that very question, and he'd beat me to it. Like he knew I would want them there. Had Asher put the thought in his head? Surely, Patrick wasn't that thoughtful. He didn't seem the type, being the all-powerful leader of Alban and whatnot.

He kept surprising me. With the election. His plan to fix things. Even restraining from biting me for my own comfort. Now, this. If he hadn't been a vampire, I'd have been close to falling in love with him.

I opened my mouth to thank him for all he'd done when the very person I'd been looking for stepped into the room. The moment Marsha's eyes landed on Patrick and me, I knew there was going to be trouble. He couldn't have possibly learned about the wedding already? Right?

The pure fury in his eyes said that yes, yes, he had.

Chapter 9

"I THOUGHT YOU WERE going to talk to him," Patrick said, his voice low.

"I was going to, but I couldn't find him," I hissed back. "Asher was a bit too good at his job."

Marsha barreled toward us so fast that Patrick and I jumped to our feet. Whatever Marsha was going to say, he stopped when his eyes landed on Patrick's warning gaze.

I stepped out from the table putting myself between Marsha and Patrick. "Hey, Marsha. I've been looking for you. I wanted to talk to you about something."

"About your wedding?" Marsha's hot gaze snapped to me and then to Patrick. "To him."

"Yeah," I swallowed and placed a hand on his chest, prepared to push him if it came to a fight. "About that. Let's go for a walk, and I'll tell you all about what Asher has planned."

At this point, we'd drawn a crowd and Marsha had noticed. It didn't keep him from shooting a glare at Patrick though as I led him out of the dining room. Before we left, I glanced over my shoulder to meet Patrick's eyes. The tight line of his jaw showed his displeasure, but the nod of his head told me he wanted me to do what I had to do.

Not that I wasn't going to anyway.

Once outside the dining room, I shoved a hand at Marsha's chest, making him wince. "What the hell was that?"

"Are you really going to marry that monster?" Marsha growled. "After what you know?"

I shook my head and frowned. "That was part of the plan in the first place. Being the convert means we become one of them. Marriage is part of that deal."

"Not for me," Marsha snapped. "Tris and I have no plans to join together in marriage. And I wouldn't now, in any case."

"Yeah, but Tris isn't the leader of Alban," I hissed. "Patrick is. It's not optional for me. The people will want us to be married before I'm converted to being in the Fold." I tried to explain what I knew to Marsha, but really, I was grasping at straws. I barely knew what was going on, let alone knowing enough to convince him that I didn't have a choice.

"But you don't have to," Marsha countered as if reading my mind. "We could leave. Together."

Shaking my head sadly, I said, "It's not that easy. Don't you think I've already thought of that?"

"But we need to get out of here. Otherwise, you're gonna be stuck with that … that …" Marsha's voice trailed off as if too angry to finish. He glared at the dining hall's door, trying to burn through it with his eyes. "Thing."

"Hey," I snapped. "You're in the same boat as me. You're just a bit late to the party. You should be worrying about your own life, not mine. Do you think Tris is just going to let you say thanks but no thank you, I don't want to be a vampire?"

"Wait, what?" Marsha's brow furrowed.

I gaped at him. "Wait, you don't know, do you?" When Marsha just stared at me, I let out a bitter laugh. "Come on." Turning on my heel, I led him toward my room.

"What's going on?" Marsha followed close behind me. "I thought we just had to be their companions, eventually spouses, not become like them!" Marsha's voice started to get louder, causing a few people to look our way.

"Would you be quiet?" I grabbed his arm, giving the onlookers a nervous smile. "Wait until we are in my room, then we can talk."

Thankfully, Marsha listened to me, and we didn't have any other outbursts. As soon as we got behind my room doors though, it was another story altogether.

"Now, will you tell me what's going on?" Marsha asked and then stopped to take in my bedroom. "Your room ..."

"Yeah." My face flushed when I realized this was the first time he'd been in it. I didn't know why it was any different than Asher or Patrick being in there, though when Patrick had been in here, I'd had a whole other reason to be embarrassed.

"It doesn't seem like you," he commented as he fingered the edge of my frilly comforter.

I shrugged. "None of this is me, but it's a place to sleep." I walked over to my nightstand and pulled out the book I'd come here for. "And plan."

"*A Guide for the Newly Converted*?" Marsha read when he took the book. Sitting down on the edge of my bed, he thumbed through it, his eyes getting wider the more he read. "How long have you had this?"

Sitting next to him on the bed, I sighed. "Since the last night of the election."

"And you didn't think I might want to read it too?" Anger colored his voice.

I snatched the book from his hands and glared. "I tried to tell you what was going on, but you blew me off. Don't blame me for your denial."

"I wasn't in denial." Marsha abruptly stood to his feet. "It was just too crazy to believe."

"Not so crazy now," I murmured.

"No." Marsha ran a hand through his hair and glared down at the ground. After a moment of silence, he said, "So, this conversion. We'll become vampires too?"

"Yep."

"And that means drinking blood, living forever, et cetera?" he raised a brow.

"Pretty much."

Scratching the back of his ear, Marsha chuckled. "In different circumstances, this would actually be pretty cool. You know, I always wished there were other things out there, but never did I think for one second, they could be real ... or ruling us."

I nodded. "It's pretty surreal."

Marsha grew quiet again. I didn't say anything. He needed time to think. It had taken me a few days to process it all too. I didn't expect him to fully comprehend the situation right away.

Pacing the floor, Marsha rubbed his chin and chewed on his lip. I about told him to go to his own room if he was going to run a hole in the carpet when he stopped and spun toward me. "Cattle!"

"Huh?"

Marsha shook his head and chuckled, the sound angry and dark. "I don't know how I didn't see it before. It all makes sense now."

"What does?" I stood and approached him.

"Don't you see it?" Marsha held his hand out. "Three rings, all circling around the core. The Glade and Middleton are the workers, they keep Alban working and fed."

"Okay?" I raised a brow.

"Then the Inner Ring, we end up with more of the food and resources, right?"

"Right."

"And only those from the Inner Ring are invited to the election," Marsha added, an expectant look on his face as if I was supposed to catch on.

I stared at him for a moment and then it all clicked. My mouth dropped open, and I felt sick. Marsha was right. We were cattle. Well, maybe not those in the outer rings but the Inner Ring, they were cows being fattened by the core to be invited to a slaughter.

"You see it too, don't you?" Marsha asked, disbelief in his voice. "It's only a matter of time before they get bored of playing human and kill us all."

"I don't think Patrick would let that happen," I said, a need to defend him becoming strong.

Marsha scoffed. "He's probably the one who orchestrated this whole thing. And you'll be his, at his side as he drains our families, our friends."

I shook my head. "No, no. Patrick wants to stop the way things are run. He and Asher brought me here for that reason."

"What do you mean brought you here?" Marsha asked, his eyes narrowing. "Are you in on all this?" he waved his hands around the room. "You get to be one of them, and all you have to do is keep the people quiet?"

"No, of course not." I snapped, unable to stop my voice from rising. "I don't know how you could think such a thing. I'm the one trying to warn people."

"Well, you aren't warning anyone in here." Marsha looked around the room. "You're just as bad as the rest of them, just letting decisions be made for you."

"And you weren't much different until last night."

"But I didn't know then," Marsha argued. "I do now. And you can let these monsters run you around under the pretense of fixing things, but I'm going to do something real."

"Oh, yeah?" I crossed my arms over my chest. "What's that? Go running through the streets shouting, 'Vampires rule Alban.'?"

"If I must," Marsha spat out, his jaw clenched.

"And what proof do you have of that?"

He opened his mouth and then shut it before he shot back, "I'll tell them what happened. What I saw?"

"And why should they believe you?" I asked, a smug satisfaction filling me. I'd thought of all this myself, after all.

"This." Marsha held up the book I'd given him. "I'll show them this."

I stared at the book. "I don't know Marsha. I don't think a book will be enough. We need real proof."

Marsha gave an aggravated sigh. "Well, unless you can hog tie a member and bring them with us, I don't see any other choice."

"We could wait and make a real plan," I reasoned.

"By then it'll be too late." The sadness in Marsha's eyes made me think he wasn't talking about us becoming vampires.

I took a step toward him. "Just don't do anything rash, okay?" I placed my hand on his chest, his heartbeat pounding beneath my hand. "I don't want to lose you."

"I don't want to lose you either." Marsha grasped my hand in his, his eyes boring into me. His face lowered toward mine, and I only had a moment to turn my face, making his lips brush my cheek.

"You should go," I whispered.

"Is this because of him?" Marsha asked, not angry but disheartened. "Do you have feelings for him?"

I shook my head. "I don't know how I feel. It would be easier if I could say yes, say something definitive. The fact is that I feel an attraction to him and to you as well." I placed my hand on his cheek. "But it wouldn't be right to let you kiss me like this."

"Why not?" Marsha smirked. "Maybe I'll win you over."

I smiled back at him. "Because when you kiss me, I want it to be because I want you to and not because you need to win me over."

Marsha didn't argue, just nodding. "I understand." Dropping my hand, he stepped back from me. "That doesn't mean I won't still fight for that date. Even if I have to stake that bastard to get it."

I opened my mouth to argue, but Marsha had already walked out the door. It wasn't until moments later that I realized he'd taken the book with him. I thought about going after him but decided not to. I'd read the book a million times. I knew it front to back. He needed it more than I did. Who knew? Maybe he'd find something to help us.

With all that was going on, we needed something substantial to help us out of this mess. I hadn't been lying when I told Marsha we couldn't just run. We'd get wiped out before we could even tell anyone. No, the best way to handle this was to be careful. We had to plan and find proof.

Marsha's idea to grab one of the Fold members came to mind. It wasn't a bad idea, but who could we grab that wouldn't be missed? Plus, they were vampires. Based on my findings, they were each ten times stronger than us. The fact that they had been able to hide their nonhuman ways so easily showed how simple it would be for them to overtake us. They'd ruled over Alban for all this time without any opposition, wasn't that proof enough?

Unfortunately, all my ideas brought me back to marrying Patrick. With my new position, I would have access to more things. I'd be able to find something we could use. Maybe even start changing things from the inside out.

If I didn't end up a vampire in the process.

Chapter 10

AFTER MARSHA LEFT, I spent the rest of the day in my room, mulling over what had happened and what should be done. When I was done thinking, I realized how little I knew about our leaders. I needed more information. Like a lot more.

I didn't even know all the names of the Fold members, let alone what their strengths or weaknesses were. When I did escape, wouldn't it make more sense to know everything about them so we could take them down?

The problem was where did I find this information? They weren't just going to hand it over by asking nicely. Or would they?

Leaving my room, I headed for the only person I knew who had all the answers I needed. Patrick. I just hoped he would give them to me without wanting anything in return.

Even though we were next door to each other, I'd never been to Patrick's rooms. Obviously, I tried to keep as much distance between us as possible, and that meant staying away from the places he resides.

I stood before his door, my hand hanging in mid-air as I prepared to knock, only to drop my hand. I started to turn back to my room thinking I'd just ask Asher but then shook my head. Where was my spine? It wasn't like he would ravish me because I was in his room.

But don't you want him to?

No, no. I glared at the floor. I'd meant what I said to Marsha. I didn't know for sure what I felt. I didn't hate Patrick, but that didn't mean I had feelings for him. He had a sort of allure to him, but I was almost a hundred percent sure that had to be the vampire thing.

Okay, eighty percent sure.

Besides, the fact that we barely knew each other he wasn't someone I could grow old with. I could with Marsha.

But you'd live forever.

What about kids? I argued. I wanted kids someday. I didn't even know if Patrick

109

could have children. Or if that part even worked anymore because of him being a vampire.

"Are you going to stand there all night?"

I jumped in place, before spinning around to find a bemused Patrick waiting a few feet away. "Can you have kids?"

Internally, I wanted to smack myself for saying that, but really, I wanted to know.

Patrick didn't seem bothered by my question. "You've been waiting out here, debating about knocking on my door, because you want to know if I can have children?" The grin on his face made me feel silly.

"Uh, no. Maybe. Just ... can you?" I huffed.

"Why? Were you thinking of having some with me?" He cocked a brow.

I ducked my head, my face heating at the thought of having children with Patrick. "Not anytime soon, but I'd like to know all my options," I finished, raising my chin higher.

Patrick placed his hands behind his back as he strolled toward me. Leaning down to meet my gaze, Patrick answered, "Then you're in luck because children are quite possible."

His nearness made my heart flutter in my throat, and I had to clear it before I said, "Good to know."

Standing back to his full height, Patrick glanced at his door and then back to me. "Did you have any other questions I could answer? We could go inside."

"No!" I shouted and then quickly added, trying to make my voice as neutral as possible. "I mean, I do have questions, yes, but no, I don't want to go in your room."

"Afraid I'll eat you?"

My eyes flashed up to Patrick's where he grinned, his eyes laughing at me.

"Yes." That one word destroyed all the humor in Patrick's face, and I instantly regretted it.

Clearing his own throat, Patrick moved around me. "Well then, we could use my office to talk. A nice neutral place, we can even leave the door open."

I followed him into his office, butterflies doing a strange dance in my stomach. Even being in his office alone put my nerves on edge. Not that I thought anything would happen. Because it wouldn't. We were just having a polite conversation about how to kill his people. See? Nothing to worry about.

Patrick's office had almost as many books as the library. They were lined along all four walls in large bookshelves. In the center of it all sat an oak desk. Patrick didn't sit behind the desk but leaned against the edge of it, gesturing to the seat in front of him.

"No thanks. I'll stand." I stayed where I was by the door.

Patrick locked eyes with me, impatience on his face. "Would it make you feel better if I sat down as well?" Patrick straightened and rounded the desk, taking a seat in the extravagant chair behind his desk.

I shrugged but sat down. Didn't want to be rude after all.

"So," - Patrick laced his fingers in front of him - "what did you want to discuss?"

Shifting in my seat, I tried to get my thoughts together enough to formulate my question. But how do I get what I want to ask out without pissing him off?

"You seem troubled." Patrick leaned forward, his brows furrowed. "Please, I want you to feel like you can ask me anything. This is a safe place."

I snorted, which made Patrick smile.

"I'm serious. We're in this together." His intense gaze was starting to make me squirm for a whole different reason.

His words, while supposed to be comforting, did the exact opposite. How could we be on the same team when we weren't the same ... anything? He and his kind fed on us. You didn't stop to have a chat with your breakfast.

Unfortunately, no matter my doubts, I did need answers and Patrick had them.

"I need information," I blurted out.

With a grin on his lips, Patrick said, "I figured."

"I mean ..." I moved to the edge of my seat. "You've got me at a disadvantage. I just found out about you and" - I swallowed - "your kind."

"Yes?" Patrick drew out.

"So, I need to know."

"Know what exactly?"

"Everything."

Patrick sat back in his chair, one elbow propped up on the side arm as he stroked his chin. "Everything is a tall order."

I shrugged. "I like to be prepared."

I tried hard not to feel guilty. Like I wasn't going to use the information Patrick might give me to turn on him and his kind, not for absolutely certain. I still wasn't sure what I'd do with it once I found out.

"Well." Patrick smacked his lips. "Where would you like to start? From the beginning?"

"That'd be a good start."

"All right. I don't know much about how we came to be. Maybe it was millions of years of evolution? Or it happened just recently after the old world fell apart. I'm not the oldest of us." He stared off into the distance as if trying to recall his memory.

"So, there are others?" I leaned on the desk, eager to hear more. "Like you, besides here in Alban I mean."

"Yes," Patrick nodded. "When the old world fell, people scrabbled amongst themselves. Fighting for resources, land, you name it. And as usual, the strong began to prey on the weak."

"The weak being us." I swallowed hard, not liking where this was going.

The inclination of Patrick's head confirmed it. "It became a slaughter. Soon, the number of humans were less than that of vampires. You know how that would have ended." He gave me a wry smile.

"No more food means goodbye vampires."

"Exactly. So, something had to change." Patrick sighed. "That is when this brilliant plan came to be." He held his hands out to each side.

My brow furrowed as I took in everything he told me. "But the people just let you corral them?"

"At first there was resistance, but when they realized they could live their lives peacefully as long as they provided us substance, they started to …"

"Get with the program. I get it." I understood what he was saying, where he was coming from, but it didn't mean I liked it. The strong were still preying on the weak, except they just didn't know it. Not yet.

Patrick didn't try to fill the quiet with words. It didn't seem to bother him like it did most humans. Maybe it was a vampire thing.

I still had questions though.

"So, the guidebook said I'd feel hungry afterward."

"Oh, you found that old thing," Patrick smirked.

"Yeah, Asher was pretty distraught about it."

Patrick smiled one of his debonair smiles that made my stomach feel funny. "Poor bastard. I'd hid it from him when he transitioned over. I'd thought I done a better job of hiding it. Apparently not."

"You hid it?" I arched a brow. "On purpose?"

"A joke between family."

"Oh, yea. Cause turning into a bloodsucking fiend completely ignorant of what was about to happen would be great fun." The sarcasm dripped from my mouth like melted chocolate.

"When you live as long as I do, you have to find your pleasures in creative ways." The way he looked at me when he said it, I had a feeling he wasn't thinking the hardy-har-har kind of pleasure.

"So, besides the obvious blood sucking ... do you have supernatural strength? Move quicker than I can blink?" I ticked them off on my fingers.

"I don't think I'm too much faster than your fellows." He grinned. "Though, I do believe I'm a bit stronger than the average human."

"So, any weaknesses?" The question came out of my mouth before I could stop it. I'd meant to be subtler about it, but Patrick didn't seem to notice my slip up.

"Not really, no." I frowned, and Patrick chuckled. "Don't look so disappointed."

"I'm not disappointed." I sat up straight in my seat.

Leaving it alone, Patrick continued, "We are a bit harder to kill than humans, but we can be killed. Cut off our heads, stab us in the heart, for example." Patrick glanced off to the side as if thinking of something. "I guess you could starve us."

"But I've seen you eat regular food."

"Oh yes, I do enjoy a good steak." Patrick grinned, a twinkle in his eye. "We don't need to eat regular food, but it does help with the cravings of having something to bite into."

I grimaced, and my hand went up to my neck until I saw Patrick watching me. I dropped my hand and ducked my head as I stood. "I think I should be going."

"What? No more questions?" Patrick met me at the door. "I could break down our basic genealogy if you'd like."

I laughed. "No, I think I'm all right. Thank you, for this." I nodded to the room.

"Not a problem." Patrick held the door open for me. "Like I said, you can trust me. I only want to help."

Smiling despite myself, I ducked my head down. "You make it so hard."

"What?" Patrick gave me a curious look.

"Hard to dislike you."

"Then I'm doing an excellent job." Patrick leaned in, brushing my hair behind my ear. My face heated at the touch of his hand.

"Uh, night," I muttered and quickly headed toward my room.

When I arrived back at my room, I knew I wasn't alone. I grabbed the lamp off my nightstand and held it in front of me. "Who's there."

A figure moved in the shadows of my room. I inched toward it, ready to swing away with the lamp if necessary. "Show yourself."

"Don't attack." Marsha stepped out of the shadows.

"Marsha." I sighed, dropping the lamp back down to the nightstand. "What are you doing here?"

"I found our proof." Marsha tugged on a rope, and an unconscious Tris fell to the ground, hogtied.

"Oh, Marsha." I gasped. "What have you done?"

Chapter 11

"WHAT THE HELL DID you do?" I hissed, trying to keep my voice low lest I wake Tris.

Marsha shrugged. "You said you wouldn't leave unless we had proof. So, here's our proof."

"And what happened to not doing something rash?" I scoffed. "How did you even get her tied up like that?" Marsha opened his mouth, but I put my hand up. "Wait, I'm not sure I want to know. The important thing is to put her back in her bed and pretend like none of this ever happened."

"What?" Marsha dropped the rope and stomped toward me. "After all I went through to get her, now you want to just drop it?"

I shook my head. "I'm trying to think rationally here. How were you planning on getting her out of here?" I waved my arms around the room and then pointed to the window. "It's not exactly a short drop."

"We'll go out through the servant's corridors." Marsha crossed his arms over his chest, a stubborn tilt to his chin.

"And what do you do when someone stops us?" I gestured to Tris. "She's not exactly easy to explain."

"I'll figure it out if it happens." Marsha stepped closer to me until we were only a foot apart. "The problem isn't getting out of the Core, it's why are you suddenly stalling. I thought you wanted to get out of here. Warn people of what's happening."

"I did. I mean, I do." I stomped my foot. "It's not that easy to just up and leave. There are things in place—"

"No, there's not." Marsha cut me off. "There's nothing in place that you can't get away from. Unless ..." Marsha stepped back and spun around the room. "You're too attached to this. Being treated like a queen. Here you mean something but back in the Inner Ring, you're less than nobody. Just the little girl from the Glade doesn't belong here or anywhere. Or maybe it's not about who you are here at all but about who is here."

My mouth dropped open, and I couldn't find the words to defend myself.

Marsha moved closer again his eyes locked on mine. "Is that it, Clara? Have you been ensnared by the monster of the castle? Is that why you don't want to leave?"

"No, of course not," I snapped, my face heating up against my better judgment.

"It is." Anger flashed across Marsha's face. "You don't want to leave your precious Patrick."

"You don't know what you are talking about," I tried to argue, even though part of me agreed with him. I didn't want to leave him, but I knew I couldn't stay.

"Well, you can't have it both ways, Clara. Either you are with the humans or with him."

"He's not like the others. And neither is Asher." I shook my head. "You can't just lump them all together."

"They're all the same. Don't you see, Clara?" Marsha grabbed me by the arms. "They're monsters. They prey on our kind and somebody has to stop them before they kill all of us."

"They wouldn't do that, not again," I spat out before I could think better of it.

Marsha's face clouded over. "What do you mean 'again'?"

I jerked my arms free from Marsha's grasp and rubbed the sting out of them. "I went to talk to Patrick, and he let me in on the history of this place."

"This place?"

"Alban and all the other ones like it."

"There are more of those monsters?" Marsha gaped.

I nodded. "And more places set up like this. Humans on the outside, working to feed the Core."

"Then we have to stop them. Free Alban, and then take on the rest of them." Marsha marched back to where Tris laid. "We should burn the lot of them. That should do them."

I sighed. "The problem with freeing everyone is that it'll turn into a slaughter. It's what caused this whole situation in the first place. The humans were becoming extinct because of the endless feeding. Now, there's a system in place."

"A system they created," Marsha snapped.

"Well, maybe it's not so bad." I hated myself for even saying it, but I didn't see any other option to fix things. I wasn't exactly sure what there was to fix. Patrick and Asher talked about making things better, but for who? Humans or them?

"So, what?" Marsha spun back around. "You want to do nothing? Let everyone go on being ignorant to the monsters controlling them? Because I can't. I won't, and neither should you."

"I know." I sighed and pulled my hair. "I just can't think of a better option. Maybe after I marry Patrick, I'll have more power. I'll be able to help us find a better option than this." I gestured a hand at Tris.

"There is no other option, Clara." Marsha's voice was low and dangerous. "And whether or not you are with me, I am taking her and getting the word out." When I frowned, Marsha's voice softened. "Don't make me have to fight you, Clara. I don't want us to be on opposite sides because we both know a war will come once the rest of Alban finds out."

Marsha was right. There was no way the people would just let this lie. Sure, there would be a few who didn't care because it didn't affect them, but a lot of them, especially the Inner Ring, once they found out what their children were being elected for, would be out with pitchforks.

My head and heart were torn in two. I understood what Marsha was saying. I couldn't be on both sides. I needed to choose, but how do you sentence your friends to death? I certainly didn't want Asher to die. Or Patrick.

I didn't think the people would bother with who I cared about when the fighting broke out. Patrick and Asher would both just be another couple of monsters to kill. The thought of seeing Patrick beheaded made my stomach sick.

Maybe if I went with Marsha now, I could stop them from getting too out of control. I could show them that not everyone was bad. They weren't all bloodthirsty fiends.

With my heart in my throat, I swallowed hard. "All right, I'll come with you."

"Good." Marsha pulled me into his arms, his large arms holding me tight. "You're making the right decision, Clara. I just know it."

"Yeah, right," I murmured into his embrace.

After a moment, Marsha released me and turned back to Tris. "We need to hurry, I'm not sure how much longer she's going to be out."

Nodding, I waited while Marsha picked Tris up in his arms bridal style. The fact that he hadn't thrown her over his shoulder like a sack of potatoes made me wonder if he cared more for her than he was leading on. Tris had bitten him, more than I had been bitten. Surely, he had some draw to her.

I didn't have time to dwell on Marsha and Tris' relationship further before we were out the door. We walked down the hallway, which seemed overly bright for what we were doing. I'd have killed for a power outage about now but remembered we weren't in the Glade. Power outages were likely something of a myth here in the Core.

"Where to?" I asked, letting Marsha lead. I'd only been to the kitchens and had spent most of my time locked up in my room since the election. I hadn't a clue where the servant's entrance was.

Apparently, Marsha did. He marched down the hall without hesitation. He looked so at ease. Like it was an everyday occurrence for him to walk down the hall with someone tied up in his arms.

I, on the other hand, was a nervous wreck. My hands were sweating, and my eyes darted around us as if someone would jump out at any moment, screaming, "Ah Hah!"

It was curiously quiet as we made our way to the other side of the castle. I'd have expected more people out and about. Though I should have been thankful. If we did get stopped, I had no clue what to say.

"Oh, we're just heading out for the evening. You know, taking in the sights. Oh, her. Don't worry about her she just got a little tired. We tied her up to keep her from flailing about."

Yeah, right. I saw that going well.

After about the fifth turn, I got impatient. "Do you even know where you are going?" I whispered harshly.

Marsha didn't stop and turn as he answered, "It's not much further."

We went down a set of stairs and made another turn. This time down a darkened hallway with only a few flickering lights. My eyes strained to see where I was going. Would be pretty sad if I tripped and gave us away because of pure clumsiness.

A dark figure leaning against the left wall caused me to halt. "Wait, Marsha," I called out quietly. "There's someone there."

"I know," he said. "He's waiting for us."

"He? Who? You told someone else about this little plan of yours? Do you not know the definition of a secret?" I hissed lowly at Marsha's back.

"I do," a familiar voice answered as we approached the figure.

"Narq?" I squinted trying to make out his fiery red hair in the shadows. "What are you doing here?"

"Helping you, of course." His white teeth flashing in the dim lighting. "Didn't think you could get out of here on your own, did you?"

Frowning, I turned to Marsha. "How much did you tell him?"

"Not much," Marsha started, before Narq cut in.

"Everything."

Ignoring my fury, Narq jerked his head toward Tris. "This the vampire?"

Ugh. Men. I swear they didn't listen at all. I told Marsha not to do anything rash, and what does he do? Kidnap his own benefactor. I tell him not to tell anyone, and what he does he do? Tells the castle gossip-monger!

I swear the next time I plan a revolution, I'm leaving the men out of it. Apparently, they couldn't be trusted.

"Did you happen to tell anyone else about this little venture? Perhaps Violet, or maybe even Zara?" I didn't even try to hide my sarcasm.

"Don't be ridiculous, Clara." Marsha shook his head. "Violet isn't in any danger. She's too compliant for Maleria to do anything to her."

I couldn't argue with him, and as much as I wanted to bring Violet with us, the fewer people involved right now, the better. There were already too many now as it was.

"Fine. Where's this exit?" I crossed my arms over my chest, realizing I wasn't going to win this argument.

"This way." Narq started down the hallway with Marsha and me in tow.

The hallway was as empty as the halls of the rest of the palace. It bugged me. This was too easy. Where was everybody?

I voiced that question out loud.

"There's a big Crimson Fold meeting tonight. Everyone is supposed to be on lockdown," Narq gestured to a window, where the full moon shined in. "They have one every full moon."

"A lockdown?" My eyes shot to Marsha. "Did you know about this?"

"Maybe … yes," Marsha said as Narq stopped us at a door.

Narq peeked his head through the door before waving us forward. The door led outside, where the lights lit up the yard. There would be no hiding out here.

We hurried our steps until we reached a large set of hedges. Darting behind the tall foliage, that sick feeling in my stomach came roaring back. Something was wrong.

I smacked Marsha on the back, looking for an outlet for my frustration.

"Couldn't you have waited until another night? How did you think kidnapping one of the key members was a good idea?" I gestured at Tris, my voice rising in pitch.

"It was too late to stop by the time I found out," Marsha growled.

"Oh, that's great." I threw my hands up. "Don't you think someone will notice!"

"Oh, they did."

Chapter 12

I KNEW IT. FROM the moment Marsha stepped out of the shadows, I knew something like this would happen. This was why you had to have a plan. Why you didn't jump the gun and go all hog tie happy on your boss.

What you get? Freaking Zara, grinning like the cat who caught the canary. Or in this case, the traitors.

"Well, what do we have here?" Zara grinned at us, her body encased in one of her ridiculous outfits. Black leather with feathers decorating the neck. Really, where did she get that crap? Didn't she realize how stupid she looked?

"Leave us alone, Zara," Narq stepped in front of us. "Don't you have somewhere to be?"

"We're on lockdown," Zara snarled. "None of us have anywhere to be but in our rooms. Somewhere none of you are at."

I shoved in front of Narq. "You're just as guilty as us, Zara. Now, why don't you just go back to your room and none of us will say a thing?"

Zara gnashed her teeth at me. "I'm not the one carrying an unconscious Fold member. And based on those ropes, I'd say she didn't come willingly."

Marsha shifted Tris in his arms, his jaw tensing. "I didn't hurt her. We're just going for a walk."

"Yeah, you are." Zara smiled viciously. Suddenly, Zara yelled, "I found her, she's over here."

Footsteps beat on the ground coming toward us, fast.

I shoved at Narq's back. "Get out of here."

"No," Narq shook his head. "I'm just as guilty as you guys."

"But you're just the help. They'll wipe you or worse." I shoved him again.

"And not you?" Narq gritted his teeth.

I barked out laughing. "Do you think they'd risk the backlash of getting rid of us? Me?"

"She's right," Zara giggled. "You're cannon fodder. They're Creme Brule. Doesn't mean I won't enjoy watching them burn though." She winked at me.

My hand curled into a fist, but I refrained from the impulse to hit her. I was in enough trouble as it was.

Narq cursed under his breath. He glanced at Marsha and me, a look of regret in his eyes before he took off into the hedges.

I sighed. At least, I was able to save one of us, even if I couldn't save myself.

The footsteps were closer now, and voices shouted as their eyes landed on us. Armed soldiers mixed with Crimson Fold members came rushing toward us. They took in Marsha and me before their eyes shifted to Tris tied up in Marsha's arms.

"Arrest them," Beaford commanded, at the head of the soldiers.

"Don't fight them," I muttered under my breath to Marsha. "It'll only make it worse. I'll get us out of this. Somehow."

"That sparks confidence in me," Marsha muttered back.

The soldiers were closing in on us, so I didn't have time to remind him that this was all his idea. The fact that I wasn't planning to throw him to the wolves should be a blessing.

I lifted my hands in front of me to show I was unarmed as the soldiers snatched Tris from Marsha before forcing him to his knees. Beaford loomed over us, a smug grin on his face.

"I knew you were bad news the moment I saw you." He sneered. "You should have taken my offer when you had the chance. Now, you'll bleed for this."

"I'd rather die," I spat as they forced me to my knees as well.

Beaford squatted next to me, his hand grabbing my chin. I struggled against him, but his grip was too strong. "Oh, you will, but not before I sink my fangs into you first."

"Beaford," Patrick's commanding voice pulled everyone's attention. "What are you doing to my fiancé?"

Beaford released me and straightened. "Your fiancé and her little friend attacked Tris and were about to escape."

Patrick came into view, his form rigid and domineering. This was not the man I had talked with in his office not too long ago. This was the leader of Alban, and I wasn't sure if that still made him my friend.

"That does not give you the right to touch what is mine."

My insides demanded me to remind him I didn't belong to him, but I'd rather be at the mercy of Patrick than Beaford any day. Beaford didn't seem to share my opinion, however. He quivered before Patrick, his mouth opening and closing like a fish out of water.

"But sire, they are traitors and should be destroyed immediately." Beaford squeaked out, squirming beneath Patrick's gaze.

"They will be brought before the Fold and judged accordingly. If found guilty, then they will be dealt with and not by you." The finality in Patrick's words seemed to keep Beaford from arguing any further. When Patrick turned his hard gaze on me, I couldn't help but wilt beneath it. There was no kindness there, no flirting smile.

Before I could try and talk to him, Patrick turned his gaze away and to the soldiers. "Bring them."

A soldier grabbed me by the arm and hauled me back to my feet. Marsha stood beside me, his body tense and shaking. I knew he wanted to shove them away. He'd already shown me that he wasn't the type to be compliant, no matter his past actions.

Whatever they decided for us, he wouldn't go easily.

And neither would I.

"I told you, you didn't belong here." Zara crooned alongside us. "Now, you are going to wish you had listened to me all along."

"Beaford!" Patrick snapped, causing the small man to rush to his side. "Control your pet before I do it for you."

"Yes, sire. Of course, sire," Beaford stuttered and nodded his head excessively. He then turned to Zara and snapped his fingers at her.

Zara sniffed and put her nose in the air but followed him like a loyal dog.

With Zara not there to taunt us, I felt better but only just slightly. We still were in over our heads, and I was having a tough time thinking of an excuse for our little excursion.

"Let me take the fall," Marsha whispered. "It was my idea after all. You just came along with it."

"No," I argued lowly, my eyes darting to the soldiers around us. "They need me more than you. If I can make it out to be my idea, cold feet and all that, maybe they'll let you go."

Marsha snorted. "You think your fiancé will just let me go? He'd take any excuse to get rid of me."

I rolled my eyes. "He would not."

"Would so. He's jealous of what you and I have." Marsha stared into my eyes. "He knows he can't make you love him like you could love me."

My mouth pressed shut. I didn't have an answer for that. I didn't love either of them. I'd never even thought of the possibility that I could, but somehow Marsha felt like he knew me better. Could I fall in love with Marsha?

Possibly. If we weren't in the middle of this mess and back in the Inner Ring.

But we weren't. I couldn't change that, no matter how much a small part of me wanted to.

Marsha was wrong about one thing though. I knew myself well enough to know that if Marsha weren't around, I'd have easily fallen for Patrick. He was funny, charming, and alluring. Heck, most of Alban's girls were already in love with him from afar. It would be hard not to fall for him, even knowing what he was.

They marched us into the castle and toward the room we had done our interviews in. I could only assume that was where the Fold had been meeting at. I'd hoped not to come back to this room. The memories I had of it weren't pleasant, and now there was no Daphne, no Asher to make my nerves go away.

Patrick pushed the doors open and led the way inside. The soldiers spilled into the room taking preassigned places along the wall and doors. The soldiers assigned to Marsha and I forced us to the ground in front of the table. Twelve chairs sat behind the table, some of them were empty. Two of them were filled by Beaford and Patrick as they took their seats. I didn't know what they had done with Tris, but her seat remained vacant.

The eyes of the Fold bored into me. Maleria shifted in her seat as if she didn't want to be here. I didn't blame her, I didn't either. The others leered at us as if we were fresh meat and they were starving animals ready to close in for the kill. Marcus's flashing fangs caught my attention the most, and I hated that I shrunk back from his gaze.

"Are these the ones responsible for Tris' absence?" a woman with short blonde hair asked, her expression more inquisitive than hungry.

Patrick glanced her way, "Yes, Katrina. Beaford found them by the servant's exit with Tris unconscious and bound."

"Then kill them," a bored tone came from a slender man with black hair braided and thrown over his shoulder. "And let us be back to our meeting."

An argument broke out amongst them. Some asking for our deaths, others wanting to feed on us. I could feel the terror seeping into me, and I searched out Patrick's gaze.

I found no solace there. They were cold and unfeeling as before. I couldn't tell one way or the other how he felt, but I could guess.

Betrayed.

I'd betrayed him and Asher's confidence. Asher would forgive me I was sure. He was more so human than Patrick. But Patrick and I had just spoken of trust, and I had so easily broken it just moments later. How could he ever forgive me for that?

"No." Patrick's clipped voice echoed through the room, a resounding sound that made them all quiet. "They will be heard and then judged. We are not animals, and we will not act like ones."

The members grumbled but settled down. Patrick motioned to one of the soldiers, and he grabbed Marsha off the ground. Dragging him toward the table, they stopped him just a foot before Patrick.

"Marsha. Why did you attack your companion?" Patrick's face might have been void of any emotion, but his voice held resentment and disgust. Maybe Marsha had been right. Was Patrick jealous?

Marsha, the big idiot, shrugged. "Seemed like a good idea at the time."

"See? An admission of guilt! You should just kill him," the man with the braid announced.

Patrick glared at him and growled, "When I want your opinion, Victor, I will ask for it." He then turned his attention back to Marsha. "And what did you intend to do with Tris once you had her at your mercy?"

Marsha didn't answer at first. Instead, he shifted in place and then glanced over his shoulder at me.

"I asked you a question," Patrick snapped. "You do not look at her. You look at me."

Even before the entire Crimson Fold, Marsha did not shy away. If anything, Patrick's words made him stand taller, his chin moving an inch higher, as if he had already known his fate.

"I planned to show her to the rest of Alban. Show them what monsters really ruled their cities." Righteous anger laced Marsha's words even as they condemned him.

The breath I had been holding as I waited for his answer blew out, and I sank further into the floor. He'd doomed himself, if not me too. I should have known better than expect him to lie. We'd be lucky to die at this point.

"And what of *my* fiancé, Clarabelle?" Patrick asked. I didn't doubt he was reminding Marsha who I belonged to. "Was she also in on your plan, or did you just decide to bring her along, this close to her wedding day?"

My head jerked up at his words. I stared at his face, trying to decipher what he was trying to say. Why would he ask Marsha about me that way?

Whatever Patrick was trying to do, Marsha seemed to catch on. "No." Marsha shook his head. "I knew Clara was feeling nervous about the wedding, so I convinced her to come with me. She didn't know anything about my plans until it was too late."

"Bull," Beaford argued. "That girl has had it in for us since the moment she stepped into the Core. You saw her interview." Beaford glanced down both ends of the table. "She hates us. Probably set this whole thing up herself."

There were a few murmurs of agreement before Patrick shut them down. "Quiet." He gestured for me to come forward and the soldier by my side pushed me to my feet. I kept my eyes on his pale ones as I stopped before him.

"Clarabelle," Patrick's voice softened. "Is what this boy saying is true?"

I opened my mouth to answer and then glanced at Marsha. The pleading looking in his eyes kept me from saying what I wanted to. To tell Patrick I'd planned to turn on him from the beginning. That I was just as guilty as Marsha. Instead, I snapped my mouth shut and nodded once, sealing both our fates.

Chapter 13

MARSHA AND I WERE taken across the hall while the Fold deliberated. The room looked the same as it did during the election minus the big table of food.

"It seems bigger," I commented after a few moments of silence. "I mean, with only us in it. I remember it being smaller."

Marsha glanced up from where he sat on the couch. "That's because there aren't dozens of prospects waiting around to be slaughtered."

I sighed and sat beside him. I glanced at the soldiers standing guard by the doors before taking his hand. "They weren't waiting for slaughter. Patrick sent them home. Memories erased. Happy as a clam."

"That's what he says," Marsha snapped. "But were they really? Or are they doing to do to us what they did to them? Maybe we'll just be drained and dumped into a ditch."

"You're the one who went all 'It's my fault in there,'" I reminded him. "You could have made up an excuse. I would have gone along with it." I squeezed his hand. "I don't want to see you hurt."

"And neither do I." Marsha held my gaze before he placed his hand on top of mine, sandwiching mine between the two of his. "But I'd rather go down for this than you, and you saw Patrick. He wants that too."

I pulled my hand from his and jumped to my feet. "Well, maybe I don't care what either of you wants? Did you ever think about that? I'm a big girl; I can take care of myself. I didn't have to go along with you, but I did." I knelt in front of him, grabbing his knees for support. "You were right. I can't stay here and wait for something to fall into my lap. We have to make the first move, even if it's the wrong one."

"Well, that's neither here nor there now." Marsha chuckled. "We already screwed up." He rubbed a hand over his face. "I should have listened to you. I'd been so hyped up on getting you out of here, I did exactly what you told me not to do."

"Getting me out of here?" I cocked my head to the side. "I thought this was about informing the people?"

Marsha locked eyes with me. "Informing the people was only partly my motivation."

"And the rest?"

"I can't let you marry him, Clara." Marsha cupped my cheek with his hand. "No matter if it's a guise. I want to be the one you walk down the aisle to, not that bloodsucker."

"Marsha," I murmured, ducking my head down to hide my blush. "I didn't realize you cared so much about me."

Marsha lifted my chin with his hand. "I've only been in love with you since the day I met you. Why else would I give you extra steaks every time you visited?"

I laughed. "Trying to buy my affections through meat?"

He shrugged. "I used what tools I had. Did it work?"

The edges of my lips drooped down.

"I'll take that as a no." Marsha sighed and stared down at the ground.

I moved closer to him until I sat between his knees. "It's not that I don't like you. I do, but love isn't something to jump into. Especially not now."

"Why not now?" Marsha countered. "If not now, when? After we're dead? Or worse, vampires?"

I shook my head. "I don't know, but I can't give my heart to someone when I'm not a hundred percent sure it's mine to give."

The hurt on Marsha's face made me wish I could take back those words. Marsha leaned away from me, his face shutting down until there was no emotion.

"Marsha," I started, trying to get some reaction from him, to see that easy going smile again. "I didn't mean-"

"Yes, you did," Marsha cut me off. "I knew you felt something for him more than attraction. I was just too stupid to see it." He turned his face away from me. "No wonder you didn't want to leave."

"Marsha, I—" But I was once again cut off when the doors to the room opened, and Patrick stepped in.

His eyes locked on Marsha and me, frowning at our position but then as quick as it came, his face resumed its icy exterior. "It's time."

Those two words didn't spark any joy inside of me, but it did tell the soldiers to come for us. I wanted to kick and scream, fight back, anything, but I knew it would be useless. Patrick could have taken us both without breaking a sweat. Who were we kidding? We weren't soldiers. Not like the half dozen coming toward us. We'd be taken down in moments.

No, I had to be smart about this. Patrick and Marsha wanted me free. If they had done their job, then I wouldn't be walking into a death sentence, and I could find a way to free Marsha. I hoped.

We were silent as we were marched back across the hall. Neither of us had anything left to say, not that would help in any case. I had a feeling Marsha was regretting saving me right about now.

They stopped us before the Fold members once more. Patrick didn't take his seat this time but stood before us.

His hands clasped behind his back, he held his head high as he spoke, "The Crimson Fold has come to a decision." Patrick lowered his eyes to meet mine. "Clarabelle, you are restricted to your room and are to be kept under constant watch until the conversion. We have decided you were acting under duress, a case of cold feet if you will." He smiled slightly, but it didn't reach his eyes.

There were a few grumbles from the table, many of them coming from Beaford.

Apparently, the vote had not been unanimous. Not surprising, Beaford had it in for me since the beginning. After my rejection, it was only natural he'd want to get rid of me.

Not before he fed on me though, I reminded myself.

Patrick shot a look at the table causing them to quiet once more. He turned his attention back to me, a frown on his lips. "The only visitors you will be allowed are Asher, myself, and an appointed servant. Any others will be charged with treason and killed on sight." He leaned forward, his voice going low. "This means the redhead."

I forced myself not to react to Patrick's mention of Narq. I didn't need to give away any more of my friends then I needed to. At least, I had Asher. He'd help me if I needed it. I just knew it.

Patrick moved back into position his eyes hard once more as he looked over my head. "Clarabelle, do you accept your punishment?"

I stared at him hard, but he didn't look at me. Gritting my teeth, I bit out, "Yes."

"Good." Patrick inclined his head. "Now, in the case of Marsha." My whole body tensed as I waited to hear what would happen to him. Would they kill him? Drain him dry or wipe his memory and send him back home?

Marsha didn't seem as worried as I was. He held himself straight as a rod, his jaw clenching the only sign of emotion. I wanted to take him in my arms and hold him. I wanted to tell him everything would be all right. I'd get him out of whatever they decided.

Patrick shifted until he was standing in front of Marsha. He locked eyes with him and said, "Marsha, you have performed an act of treason. You have attacked and held a Crimson Fold member against their will. That alone would have you killed."

I gasped and took a step toward Marsha, but a hand gripped my arm. I glared up at the soldier standing there. He didn't even acknowledge me, just held me back.

"Be that as it may." Patrick glanced to me and then to the table where for the first time I noticed Tris sitting in her seat. A cruel sort of grin covered her lips, and I realized whatever they had planned would be worse than whatever I could have imagined.

"Your companion, despite your actions, still wishes to have you by her side. For whatever reason," Patrick muttered and then said louder, "You will be imprisoned for thirty days."

I relaxed slightly. They weren't going to kill him. He'd live. I could save us if he lived.

This time, I wouldn't make the mistake of hesitating. If I could get one of the Fold and escape, I would. Even without one, if I could get Marsha and leave, that would be enough for me. Oh, and Narq. I couldn't leave him behind, not with him being on Patrick's radar.

I shouldn't have been planning our escape. I should have known better than to think it would be that easy. Things were never simple when it came to them.

Patrick waited as if to be sure I wasn't going to make a scene before continuing, "During that time, you will be wiped of your memory. You will not remember what you have seen or heard here while at the Core, nor will you remember anyone by the name of Clarabelle, ever again." Patrick's eyes locked with mine as he said the final words.

Those words broke me. My heart ripped in two as tears streamed down my face. I screamed, and like a rampaging animal, I shoved against the hands on me. The soldier wrapped them around my waist and pulled me back as I tried to get to Marsha. But he wasn't strong enough. A second and third soldier captured my arms keeping me from me moving more than an inch.

Patrick continued to talk as if I weren't thrashing around next to him. I didn't hear it over the beating of my heart, my blood pumping at such a rapid pace that I feared I might pass out. The words 'nor will you remember' kept running through my head.

How could he do this to me? Killing us would have been less cruel. But when was I going to learn? They weren't human. Cruelty was their specialty.

The soldiers dragged me away from the center of the room and toward the door. I could barely see through the blurring of my vision, but I could make out the gleeful grins of Beaford and Tris. I added them to the top of my list. They'd be the first to die. I had no doubt this had been their doing.

As I plotted my revenge, I found Marsha once more. Marsha's stone exterior broke as he watched me go. Agony washed over his face, and I knew he agreed with me.

This was worse.

Far worse than anything they could have done to us. I might not have loved Marsha like he loved me, but I could have. Now, any chance of that happening was gone. I'd never see Marsha smile at me again. His laughter would be for someone else.

I cursed at myself for not letting him kiss me before. Now, I'd never be able to. He wouldn't even know my name, let alone how he felt about me.

That only proved Marsha's point. Patrick had been jealous, and he'd found a way to get rid of Marsha once and for all. He'd never have to worry about him trying to steal me away from him. But he'd messed up because by taking Marsha away from me, he'd made me hate him.

Any chance that I could have fallen for Patrick had disappeared. Now, all that Patrick was to me was my captor, and I would do anything to break free.

Chapter 14

THE SOLDIERS SHOVED ME into my room and shut the door behind them. Immediately, I tried to open it only to find it locked.

Of course.

I spun back around and glared at the room. I took in the four-poster bed and the wardrobe of clothes. The food tray from dinner still sitting on the table. Anger boiled inside of me. I hated it. All of it.

I ripped the covers off the bed and threw them to the floor. I chucked the pillows at the walls, and they bounced off without a sound. Unsatisfied with the damage I'd done, I reached for the lamp on the nightstand and smashed it against the bedroom door. The glass shattered and fell to the ground.

I vaguely heard voices out in the hall but didn't care. I was on a mission. Moving over to the wardrobe, I grabbed the back of it and tried to push it over, but it was too heavy. I grunted and shoved at it, causing the insides to fall out of it.

The door to my room opened, but I ignored it. My palms became slick making it harder to hold onto the wardrobe. An arm wrapped around my waist and pulled at me. I dug my fingers into the wardrobe, determined to get it knocked over.

"Clarabelle," Patrick's voice growled in my ear, and for a moment, my grip loosened. It was enough for him to get me away from the wardrobe. He tossed me aside, and I fell to the ground.

Glaring up at him from the floor, I snapped, "What the hell do you want? Do you have something else you want to take from me?"

Patrick just stared down at me, an impatient look in his eyes. "You are acting like a child."

"He was right, you know," I snapped, crawling to my feet. "You were jealous. You were just waiting for a chance to get rid of him, and now you have it."

"Damn right, I was." Patrick snarled, closing the distance between us. "He was going to get you killed, after everything Asher and I have done to get you here." Patrick grabbed my arms keeping me from running away. "I wasn't going to lose you."

"I'm not yours to lose." I jerked against his arms, but he was too strong. I should have run when I had the chance.

"No," Patrick sighed and released me. "But you could have been. This was the only way I knew I could keep you alive, and if that meant taking him away from you, then" - Patrick paused and locked eyes with me - "I would do it again in a heartbeat."

"What do you know?" I snapped. "You don't even have a heart."

"Yes, I do," Patrick corrected me, but when I tried to dismiss him, he grabbed my hand and placed it on his chest. It raced beneath my palm and some of my anger dissipated.

I jerked my hand away and glowered. "I don't care. As far as I'm concerned, you're dead to me."

"But you aren't to me." Patrick shook his head. "Not yet."

I expected him to yell at me some more, but he turned and headed for the door. My blood was still pumping, and I couldn't just let this lie.

"You can't just walk away from me like that." I stomped after him and grabbed his arm. "You could have saved him and me. You didn't want to."

Patrick stopped but didn't turn to face me. "You're right. I didn't. I'll admit I wanted him out of the way. Out of your way." He slowly twisted to face me, disappointment in his eyes. "But that doesn't dismiss the fact that you deliberately went behind my back and took matters into your own hands. What were you thinking?"

"I was thinking I didn't want to get married or turned into a vampire," I snapped. "And Marsha was at least doing something, not just twiddling his thumbs waiting for the ones in charge to let him know when things could change."

"Is that what you think I was doing? Bidding my time?"

"Isn't it?" I accused. "You have all this power, power you used tonight. Beaford almost wet his pants, and you can't use that power to change things? You need a little girl from the Glade to do it?" We were inches from each other now.

"I can't just snap my fingers and make things better. It doesn't work that way."

"You sure fooled me," I scoffed. "I think you don't want people to know what you really are. That they would turn on you the moment that they do. And you know what? They should."

"You're right," Patrick interrupted me. "They should. We've lied and cheated to get our way, but you know what? It's worked for the last five hundred years. That's not something you change overnight."

"Why not?"

Patrick let out an exasperated noise. "You're not going to drop this, are you?"

I crossed my arms over my chest and glared at him.

He smiled wryly. "Of course not." He turned and opened the door. "Fine. Come with me."

Frowning, I hesitated to follow him. Patrick waved me forward with an impatient jerk of his hand. Inching forward, I searched the hallway. The soldiers from before were gone, leaving us alone.

"I thought I was restricted to my room."

Patrick shrugged one shoulder. "I'm making an exception."

"Why?" I arched a brow.

"To teach you a much needed lesson." Patrick started down the hall, not waiting for me to follow. After what happened, I didn't have the energy to try and run. Besides, he would catch me before I even got two feet. Part of me was tempted lock myself in my room, but my curiosity got the better of me, making me jog to catch up with him.

"What lesson do I need to learn?" I asked as he took me toward a part of the palace I hadn't been to before.

Patrick gave me a meaningful look over his shoulder. "One I should have given you when you first got here, but that was before I knew you needed it."

We walked in silence until we started to descend a set of stairs. They seemed to go on forever, and my skin began to crawl. Whatever he was going to show me I had a feeling I wasn't going to like.

"Where are we going?" I asked, but Patrick didn't answer. I grabbed his shoulder, stopping him in place.

"It's not much further. Just trust me." Patrick paused and then shook his head. "Though, I guess tonight proved you can't, can you?"

Guilt ate at me. Patrick had told me to trust him repeatedly, and I had said I would, but I really hadn't. I'd trusted Marsha over him and look where that got me. Though, I still thought he could have done more for Marsha. I should be happy we were alive at all.

I let Patrick lead me further down a hallway, my guilt and confusion making my stomach hurt. I wished things were back to the way they were in the Glade. I knew my place and where my life was going. There were no guys in sight to make me an emotional mess.

I didn't know what was right and what was wrong anymore. I thought Marsha was right, and in a way, he had been, but Patrick was also right. My head swarmed like a hive of buzzing bees, and all I wanted was something to make them stop.

"In here." Patrick stopped before a door. It wasn't a remarkable door. Just ordinary. There wasn't a nameplate or anything to tell me what was inside, nor was there any sound coming from inside.

"What's in there?" I stared hard at the door as if it could answer my question.

Patrick gave me a little shove toward the door. As my hand turned the knob, Patrick said, "This is why you have to play it my way."

The first things I noticed on the other side were the beds. They ran up and down in neat little lines. Most of the beds had someone lying on them. Either sleeping or just sitting. Some were even talking to themselves. None of them were interacting with each other though.

"There has to be a hundred ..." I murmured to myself as I stepped into the room.

"More," Patrick said in my ear, making me jump.

I walked down the aisles, taking in each person. It was like they were in a daze, their eyes glossy, not really seeing in front of them. I stopped in front of one of the beds where a girl sat. Her gray shirt and pants were clean and pressed as if they had just come out of the wash. She didn't even flinch or glance up when I came close.

Waving a hand in front of her face, she didn't so much as blink. "What's wrong with them?" I asked, glancing up at Patrick.

Tucking his hands into his pockets, Patrick gestured his head toward the girl. "They've been wiped. Some more than others."

"Why?" I stood to my feet and searched the room for an answer. "Why are they here? Why not send them home?"

Patrick met my gaze. "This is what happens to humans who know too much to let live. They get wiped and put here. This is where you and Marsha were headed, had I not intervened."

I scanned the room, still not knowing what it was about the place that bothered me so. "But why here? Why not just kill them?"

Pale eyes met mine. Patrick raised a brow, and it clicked. I looked back at the girl. Really looked at her. There, on her neck. Two small puncture holes. Closed over but there. I rushed over to her and picked up her wrist. Her arm looked like a pack of animals had attacked it. Bite marks lined up and down the inside of her arm.

"This is the feeding room," I gasped, dropping her arm and turning back to Patrick. My stomach rolled, and I swore I would be sick right there.

"Can't waste perfectly healthy food by killing them," Patrick voiced what I'd been thinking. "After all, they had it coming."

My eyes snapped to him as my anger flared to life once more. Before I could get a word out, something from the corner of my eye caught my attention. Brow furrowed, I pushed past Patrick my feet moving faster as what I'd seen came into focus.

"Tillie," I cried, falling to my feet in front of her.

Tillie didn't even see me. Her blonde hair cascading down her like a waterfall covering her shoulders and back. She wore the same gray outfit as everyone else except she had far fewer bite marks decorating her skin.

"I thought you sent her home," I accused, tears making my throat clog up. "Why didn't you send her home?"

Patrick approached slowly. He didn't touch me, which was wise. I didn't trust myself not to kill him on the spot for what he did to Tillie.

"While some are here for treason, others" - Patrick shook his head sadly - "have simply been wiped too many times. Your friend was one of them."

"And whose fault is that?" I hissed, holding Tillie closed to me. "She wouldn't have been wiped if you hadn't kept inviting her.

Patrick held his hands open. "I wasn't the one who kept inviting her."

"Is this some kind of sick joke for you?" I continued ignoring his admission. "Keep inviting her back for the chance of being elected, but then reject her so you can wipe her just so she would end up here?"

There was guilt on Patrick's face. He knew this had happened and hadn't told me until now. It had probably happened before. I wouldn't put it past them. They were all sadistic monsters.

"This is why I kept it from you," Patrick said, his voice low. "These are the kind of things I want to stop. I knew what was happening to this girl, and I couldn't do anything about it."

"Why not?" I asked, moving away from Tillie. "Why couldn't you have put your foot down and said no. That's enough. Either make her your companion or leave her alone."

Patrick's shoulders slumped. "It's in the laws."

"What laws?"

"When we made this place, we had to put laws in place, not just for the humans but for us as well. One of those laws was that each member could invite one person of their choosing. I chose you." He held his hand out to me, but I ignored it, looking back to Tillie.

"Who chose her?" I bit out. "Who was the sick bastard who did this to her?"

Patrick sighed and dropped his hand. "It's getting late. Let's go back to your room."

"No," I shouted, grabbing him by the front of his shirt and he let me. "You owe me this. You have to tell me who did this to her.”

A tortured look in his eyes, Patrick breathed out a name I will remember until the day I died, “Marcus.”

Chapter 15

IT'S BEEN DAYS SINCE our visit to the feeding rooms - somewhere I hoped never to visit again - and I'd been stuck in my room the entire time. Every time I tried to leave, a guard was waiting for me.

I knew this was part of my punishment, but it was grating on my nerves. I hadn't seen anyone but servants who only came to bring me food or take my food trays away ... or clean up the mess I made on the first night of my sentencing.

Patrick made me promise not to throw a fit again, but I was just two seconds away from tossing that promise right out the window along with my food tray. Even Asher hadn't visited.

Hell, I'd be happy just to see the chittering girls at this point. Anything to get my mind off what I saw down in the basement.

Those vacant expressions. The unblinking eyes. I could have done anything to them, and they wouldn't have put up a fight, which was probably the intention.

Any old nightmares I'd had were replaced with new ones. I was down there, but this time I was one of the occupants. The gray outfit itched, but I couldn't scratch at it. I knew something was wrong, but my head had too much fuzziness in it for me to collect my thoughts.

What was even worse was that each night, someone different visited me. Fed on me. First, it was Patrick, which did not bring happy feelings like the first time. It made my already boiling hatred molten hot and the urge to punch him in the face overwhelming if I ever saw his face again.

The worst nights were when Beaford or Marcus had me at their tender mercies. Those nights, I woke up screaming, causing the guards to rush in, guns at the ready. But after the first few times, they stopped coming, leaving me alone in the dark with my sweat covered clothes. Hot showers did nothing to warm the chill in my bones on those nights.

I'd have begged for someone, anyone, to talk to, but the servants only glanced my way before ducking out of the room. They were probably under orders not to speak to me.

One saving grace was the television in my room. Those shows I used to despise were my only means of entertainment. The news talked about my upcoming nuptials which they told me were in only a few days' time. Not that I would know. I'd been left out of the loop as far as planning went. The images they used of me when talking about it were from the election, many of them from moments I didn't even know they were filming. They even had a picture of Patrick kissing me the night he had nicked me. Of course, they left out the last bit where I ran away screaming.

A knock on my door pulled my attention from the television. I didn't have to tell whoever it was to come in, they'd come on their own. My stomach rumbled at the prospect of food, so I turned the television off and sat at the table.

The door opened, and a gasp filled the room, "Oh, dear. Oh, dear." My head jerked up to meet Venna who scurried across the room with my tray in hand. "Just look at you. Have you even bathed today?" Venna's gray head of hair bobbed up and down in front of me as she took in my pajamas from three nights ago.

"Hello, Venna," I smiled, the first one in days. It made my cheeks hurt from disuse. "Are you even allowed to talk to me?"

Venna huffed. "Those Fold members think they are all high and mighty, but I'm not about to make you or me miserable by pretending you don't exist." She went to my wardrobe and pulled a pair of pants and a blouse out. "Take those clothes off and put these on. Then you are going to eat everything on that tray and tell me all about what happened."

I didn't even hesitate to do as she commanded. She had that motherly way about her. It made it close to impossible to disobey.

With fresh clothes on, I did feel better. I probably should have taken a shower first, but still, it was good. Sitting back down at the table, I tore into the bread on my plate.

Venna sat across from me her watchful gaze on me as I ate. "I heard rumors, you know."

I arched a brow, my mouth too full to answer.

"Rumors you and a certain beefy young man were caught running away."

I swallowed hard, taking a drink from my glass. "Apparently, the Fold isn't all-powerful after all."

Venna smiled. "I believe you have your friend Narq to thank for that."

I groaned. "I should have known." Leaning back in my seat, I sighed. "How much has he told everyone?"

Venna lifted a shoulder. "Not much, just that you two were causing a ruckus and our dear leader locked that particular young man up because he was jealous."

"He's still locked up?" I asked, moving to the edge of my seat. "Have you seen him?"

With a coy grin, Venna said, "Why do you care? You're getting married in a few days."

I scoffed. "So, I've been told. The whole of Alban knows more about my wedding than me. I'm just expected to attend."

"Well." Venna leaned forward. "I heard from a little birdie that you are going to be called on soon."

"Really?" I asked. "What for?"

"Dress fittings."

Now I really groaned. "They let me out of this hell hole only to put me in another one."

Venna laughed. "This is hardly a hell hole."

"Until you're stuck in it for an undetermined amount of time." I glanced around the room with distaste. "Then it's a big putrid pile of cow dung covered in fluffy velvet pillows."

"Well, it shouldn't be much longer, then you'll be a married woman." Venna gave me a sly smile. "Is your family going to come?"

"Uh, I don't know." Before I tried to escape, Patrick had told me I could invite them, but with everything the way it was, I wasn't sure if that was still an option. The thought of my family did give me an idea though. "Venna?"

"Oh no." Venna shook her head. "I don't like that look. You're going to ask me to do something I'm not supposed to, aren't you?"

"Possibly," I smirked.

"Good." Venna leaned forward, a conspiratorial gleam in her eyes. "What do you need me to do?"

"I need you to get a message to my father." When Venna gave me an inquisitive look, I continued. "Look, my family has probably already been invited to the wedding, and if not, I'll work my way on Asher or Patrick and get them invited. That way he has a reason to be here."

"But what do you need them for?" Venna asked.

"I need to get out of here." A knock on my door interrupted me from going further. "There's too much to explain. Just tell him that I changed my mind. He'll know what I mean." I barely got the words out before the door opened and Asher stepped in.

A sneer crept across my face. "Look who decided to show his face."

Asher dipped his head, a contrite look on his face. "I tried to come sooner, I did."

"I'm sure." I stood and crossed my arms over my chest. Venna took my tray and headed toward the door, shooting Asher a chastising frown.

When Venna shut the door behind her, Asher came rushing toward me. I held my arms up defensively, not sure what he was going to do. When his arms wrapped around me in a tight embrace, I relaxed.

"I thought you were going to die," Asher muttered into my head.

Hugging him back, I chuckled dryly. "You can't get rid of me that easily. Worse have tried."

"Really?" Asher released me, a curious grin on his lips.

I smiled and shrugged. "Well, no, but it sounded good." We stepped away from each other, and I frowned. "I guess you being here means it's time to take my lickings."

"What?" Asher's brow furrowed.

"Dress fittings."

"Oh, yes." Asher smirked. "The torture will be commencing shortly. We really should get going, or we'll be late."

I rolled my eyes. "Couldn't have that, now could we?"

Asher chuckled and curled my arm around his. "It really isn't as bad as you are making it out to be. I've already done all the initial planning. We went through five different fabrics before we found the right one. We just need you to try it on for the final measurements."

"But don't you have my measurements?"

"This is your wedding dress, not a ball gown." I gave him a pointed look. "All right, so it's not that much different but still. Don't you want to see it before the big day?"

I grimaced. "Can't I just skip all that?"

Asher paused mid-step and turned to me. "We could go back to your room if you'd prefer?"

"No," I shouted and then flushed. "No, dress fitting sounds like a wonderful idea."

"That's what I thought." Asher chuckled. "Now, why don't you tell me about how you've been?"

"You mean besides being locked in my room for the last week?" I quirked a brow at him.

Asher frowned. "Okay, wrong question. Obviously, you're not okay. I heard what happened to Marsha."

"Have you seen him?" I quickly asked, and then lowered my voice when we attracted looks. "I mean, have they done it yet?"

When Asher didn't immediately answer me, I knew it was too late. My eyes burned with unshed tears. "Oh, my god. Marsha is probably sitting all alone in a cell right now with no idea who I am or why he was here. And here I was, whining about being trapped in my room."

"You can't blame yourself." Asher squeezed my arm. "He did this to himself."

"No, Patrick and his group of sadistic monsters did," I snapped, pulling my arm from his grip.

"You can't blame Patrick for this. You and Marsha could both be dead right now." Asher tried to reassure me, but he didn't know I knew there were worse options.

"No, we'd be in the feeding room."

Asher's eyes widened, and he stopped in his tracks. "How do you know about that?"

"Tell me something." I spun around, my anger suddenly billowing forth. "Do you go down there? Is that why you don't have to feed on your girls? Because you have willing, well, brain dead would be more accurate."

Asher looked down at the ground and then back to me. "I'm not going to feel bad about keeping myself alive. This is the way it has been for years. Would you rather me feed on someone who was terrified?"

"No," I quipped, "but feeding on someone who can't decide for themselves is just wrong. Especially since they are only like that because of you guys in the first place." I started to turn and then stopped, spinning back around. "And you know, I've been bitten before. I don't see the big deal. I'm sure there would be plenty of people who would line up to be your breakfast."

Asher snorted. "Yeah, and then they get addicted, and you don't know who is hanging around you because they like you or because they want you to take a nibble."

"Oh." I frowned, my anger starting to fade. "I didn't think about that."

"Well." Asher forced a grin. "You've still got years of experience to catch up on before you know everything about us."

Chapter 16

THE WEDDING DAY ARRIVED sooner than I expected. After the dress fitting, I'd been confined to my room once again. I still hadn't seen any hide or hair of Patrick.

"You think the groom would want to dote on his blushing bride," I grumbled to myself over my scrambled eggs.

"What was that?" Asher asked from where he stood with the girls, getting my things ready.

"Nothing," I said, shaking my head.

"You need to eat something," Willow urged, sitting down across from me. "You'll regret it later."

"I can't eat." I threw my fork down. "My stomach is all mixed up."

Willow smiled. "That's just the nerves. Believe me, if you don't eat something now, you won't get around to it after the wedding. My cousin, Mia, well, when she got married, she was starving by the end of the reception. She ended up spending the better part of her honeymoon scarfing down a whole turkey on her own."

My lips curled up in disgust. "Sounds greasy."

"Why didn't she eat at the reception?" Rosel asked, looking up from the lace she had been straightening out.

Willow glanced over at her. "Too many people wanting to congratulate her. Plus, there was the dancing and the cutting of the cake. All the traditional things you do at a wedding."

"Well," I coughed, "I don't think we'll be doing those things -"

"Oh yes, you will." Asher cut me off. "And more. Patrick and the rest of the Fold really want this to be a big deal. The works." I gave him a disbelieving look. "Don't look at me. They think it will help give the people something to cheer for. A big fairytale wedding, ending with the rags-to-riches princess getting everything her heart desires."

I snorted. What I desired wasn't something I could have televised to the whole of Alban. What I wanted included blood and carnage, starring many of those the very Fold members who were forcing me into this debacle in the first place. I still wasn't sure if Patrick was one of those.

Forcing a few more bites into my mouth, I gave Willow a forced smile, my cheeks full of food. She wrinkled her nose at me before returning to the preparations.

Swallowing to get rid of the food that tasted like ash in my mouth, I grabbed my glass and took a drink. Orange juice. Blech. I was so tired of orange juice. No matter how much I tell them to stop sending it, they keep doing it. Must be their idea of torture.

Asher shot me a warning glare. "Cute." He waved a hand at me. "Why don't you go shower? It will help you relax. Then we can get you ready."

Setting my fork down with a loud clack, stood from the table. Stripping my clothes off as I went, I padded into the bathroom. Turning the shower on, I stepped in.

Asher was wrong. The hot water did nothing to calm my nerves, but it did relax my muscles. I let the water wash over me, washed my hair and body because it was expected. Couldn't have a dirty bride, now could we?

I had hoped to get down to see Marsha before today, but that hadn't happened. Other than letting me out with Asher for my dress fitting, the guards hadn't let me out of my room. Venna had been absent as well.

I didn't know if she got my message to my father or not. I did find out they were coming though. Him, my stepmother, my stepsisters, the whole family. They were supposed to be here at any moment. I half hoped to see them before the wedding.

Even Julianna.

But I doubted it. I'd be a prisoner until the day I died and became a vampire. Who the heck knew when that would be?

"Are you going to stay in there all day?" Neeka asked, peeking her head into the bathroom. "You're going to get pruny."

Sighing, I turned the water off and stepped out of the shower. Taking the towel offered by Neeka, I wrapped it around my body. Neeka led me back into my bedroom where they dried me off and helped me into my undergarments.

They were silky and felt good against my skin, but they might as well have been made of sandpaper. Then their feel would have matched my feelings about them.

Rosel pinned my hair up out of the way before leading me over to the dress they had made for me. A slip covered most of my important parts. Over that was a lace made of the finest spider silk thread. It clung to my form, hanging off my shoulders and cascading down to the floor. Slit open at the knees, the skirt spread out around my legs like a cap. The shoes were open-toed but thankfully short-heeled.

"I'd hate you to trip and tear such a masterpiece," Asher commented when I slipped the shoes on.

I smiled. "And I thank you."

"You don't like it?" Rosel asked, confusion on her face. "I think it's the most beautiful thing I'd ever seen."

Shaking my head, I said, "It's not the dress, just the reason behind it."

The girls exchanged a look before Willow spoke, "Arranged marriages are not uncommon even in the Glade."

"I know," I sighed.

"And Patrick is quite handsome," Neeka added.

"I know." This time it came out sharper.

"You could have been stuck with Beaford," Rosel reminded me.

"I know!" I spun around and glared at the three who stepped back as if I'd hit them. Asher tsked at me as I stepped down from the little dais they had set up and sat down

179

at the vanity. "I'm sorry. I know my situation could be worse, but you must understand. No matter how nice Patrick is, or handsome, or how much worse it could be, none of that makes up for what he has done to my friends and me."

Before the girls could gush even more, my bedroom door burst open. In poured Lea and Julianna followed closely by their mother, Belinda. My stepsisters took one look at me in my dress and squealed with delight.

Belinda, good old reliable, sniffed and said, "I hope you are going to do something with your hair?"

Ignoring her, I searched behind them for my father, but he sadly did not show. "Where's father?"

"Mr. Blordril invited him to drink in his office," Lea answered, her eyes still wide as she danced around me. "This is so pretty. Mother, I want my dress to be just like this when I get married."

"Of course, my darling." Belinda nodded, ever the doting mother. Too bad she'd never been that way to me.

"It's all right," Julianna waved a hand at me, clearly pretending to be unimpressed. "Too much skin in my opinion."

Asher thankfully came to my rescue. "Ladies, I haven't introduced myself to you yet. I'm Asher, Clara's stylist and guide in all things of the Core." He took my stepmother's hand, kissing the back of it like a true gentleman.

"You're going to want to wash that," I told my stepmother, earning me a glare from Asher.

He did the same for both my stepsisters. Julianna blushed prettily as she had trained herself to do. Lea giggled and spun in place, not quite old enough to know how to deal with the attention.

"It's a pleasure to meet you." Belinda nodded and then gestured to me. "We've loved what you have been doing with Clarabelle's look. We hardly recognized her on the television."

"Yeah, so much better than those boots and dirty pants she always wears." Lea crinkled her brow at me.

Sighing, I turned to the girls. "Can we do my hair now?"

Thankfully, they were more than happy to oblige. They grabbed their tools and started to apply my make up while at the same time pulling my hair this way and that. My stepsister chattered in my ear the entire time, commenting about how they saw this or that on their way to the Core.

"You should see the dresses I have now," Lea cooed. "None of them are as nice as this, but they are better than the ones mother made for me." She leaned forward, her face in her hand.

"Don't brag, Lea." Julianna smacked her on the arm. "It's not becoming. Besides, we could be living in the palace soon, if we have our way." She shared a secret smile with her mother.

My stepmother sat on the side, unusually quiet as she watched her daughters brag about how their lives had changed. I'd done a great service for my stepfamily apparently. Not that they cared what it cost me.

When it was finally time to leave for the ceremony, Belinda pulled me aside. Asher and the girls looked at me with concern, but I gestured with my head for them to go. I'd handled vampires, I could handle one wicked stepmother.

"Your father is worried about you."

My eyes widened at her admission. "And you're not?"

Belinda laughed. "I know your type. Hard exterior, even harder interior. You pretend to be soft, but you are a master manipulator. I've known from the beginning. Do you think I don't know you are the reason your father had been so hard to get to propose? His little girl isn't prepared for a mother." She mimicked my father's voice.

I frowned at her. "I don't know what you are talking about. My father loved my mother, it was him that couldn't let go."

"Think what you want." Belinda snorted, a sound I'd never heard come from her. "My point is, you need to use that skill now. Whatever it is you must do to keep Patrick Blordril happy, you will do. Ride into the sunset and have your happily ever after."

My teeth gritted at her words, and I stepped closer to her until our breath mingled. "You don't know what the hell you are talking about, or what is going on in this place."

"I know that you somehow attracted the most powerful person in all of Alban, which has benefited us greatly. We have respect, endless coins. Your sisters have their pick of admirers. They could even have one of the other members of the Fold. I hear Marcus is looking for a companion." I laughed at her mention of the people at the top of my kill list. My laughter only made Belinda angry. She grabbed my arm, her nails biting into my skin. "You will not ruin that for them or me."

I laughed again, this time bitterly. "That's all you care about, isn't it? Your own rise in status. Never mind the fact that we have monsters running our world." I twisted my arm until I grabbed Belinda's arm instead. Pulling her close, I growled, "We are cattle. Nothing more than cattle to these people and you would do well to remember that before offering up any of your precious daughters to them."

Shoving her away, I marched toward the bedroom door. Stopping just at the entrance, I turned back to Belinda, "There's no such thing as a happily ever after. Not for any of us."

Chapter 17

I WAS GOING TO be sick. The further we got down the hall and toward the large ballroom where the big event was going down, the sicker I felt.

"Wait, wait." I halted in the hallway, Asher at my arm. He stopped beside me, a concerned look on his face. My stepsisters had already gone ahead, and my father supposedly was waiting for me at the ballroom doors.

"What is it?" Asher led me to a seat near a window. "What's wrong?"

I shook my head and swallowed thickly. "I can't do this." I locked eyes with him, desperation pouring out of me in waves. "I don't want to get married. Not now, not to Patrick. Maybe not ever."

Asher sighed and adjusted a lock of my hair behind my ear. "I understand how you feel, Clara. This isn't the ideal situation for any of us, but if we want to make sure the Fold isn't aware of what we have planned, we have to play our parts."

"But that's just it. What do we have planned? I don't know anything but what you and Patrick have told me." I waved my hands wildly in the air, my heart pounding in my heart so hard I swore I might be having a heart attack.

"You are still thinking like a human." Asher gave an exasperated growl. "This isn't a short game plan." He rubbed his hand over his face, his brow scrunching together. "You can't change hundreds of years of laws overnight. It takes planning … patience."

"I understand that, but why does it matter if I'm married to Patrick or not?" I waved my bouquet in the air, the flowers bouncing angrily.

"It's a show," Asher explained. "There's one thing that vampires love almost as much as blood, and that's a good show. You play your part, be the dutiful little wife. Make them think we are playing by their rules, and then we slowly start to make changes." I opened my mouth to argue. "By the time they notice that anything has changed, they won't even want to fight it."

"And what about the people down in the feeding room?" I countered. "They just stay there, mindless zombies for them to be fed on while their families wonder if they will ever see them again?"

Asher frowned. "No plan is perfect. We can't save everyone right now. We can only do what we can to make sure future generations don't share the same fate."

I turned my face away from him, glaring out the window. There were people on the lawn, more than usual because of the wedding. Cameras pointed toward the palace as reporters let the rest of Alban know what was going on. There would more than likely be even more cameras inside the ballroom. They'd make sure to get every painful detail of the whole event, making it near impossible to relax.

Asher had a point, but I didn't agree completely. I understood and even agreed that jumping into anything too fast was going to make it hard to get the other members on board. I could see an especially large amount of rebellion from Beaford and Marcus. It might just be easier to kill the lot of them.

I said as much to Asher.

Asher glowered at me. "You shouldn't say such things where anyone could hear you. Besides, it wouldn't help. You kill one member, and someone from another area would come to take their place. They always have to have a balance of twelves."

"Why?"

Standing to his feet, Asher shrugged, "How should I know? I'm barely a vampling to these people. What they find to be necessary is ridiculous and exhausting. I've found that just going with it will save you from a lot of headaches." He offered me his hand, and I reluctantly took it allowing him to lead me once more down the hallway.

"What's going to happen after the wedding?" I asked, my father coming into view.

"There will be a reception like I said before, and then you and Patrick will have a ..." Asher paused to clear his throat and then finished a bit awkwardly, "... honeymoon."

"A honeymoon!" My voice became shrill and bounced off the walls making my ears ring. "I didn't agree to that."

"Don't worry," Asher patted my hand. "Patrick will not touch you unless you wish it."

"Well, I won't," I assured him. "Not ever."

Asher gave me a wink and a smile. "That's what they all say."

We stopped before the double doors leading to the ballroom, and my father stood there, his hands wringing in front of him. Before he could even greet me, I wrapped my arms around him. I'd missed him so much in my time in the Core. I regretted every day not leaving with him while I could.

"My Clarabelle," my father crooned in my ear and leaned away to look at me. "You are as beautiful as your mother was on our wedding day."

Blushing but grinning broadly, I laughed. "You only say that because of all of Asher's hard work. Without him, I'd have ended up wearing a feed sack."

"And you'd still be the most beautiful woman here." Asher chuckled. "I hardly did anything at all. A bit of lace, a pin or two there. See? Nothing at all, really."

I shook my head at Asher's false modesty. I had an inkling it was for my father's benefit. Either way, I was still happy to have had him by my side this entire time. I would have been lost without him.

"Are you ready?" my father asked, glancing between Asher and me.

I shot Asher a look, and he returned it with a squeeze of my hand before pressing his lips to my cheek. In my ear, he whispered, "You will do fine. Just remember to breathe."

Nodding to him, Asher released me and left me alone with my father. As soon as I was sure, Asher was out of hearing distance, I moved closer to my father, grabbing his arms in desperation.

"We don't have much time. Did you get my message?" I searched his face, which I noticed had aged a lot more than the last time we'd seen each other. Had that been my doing? Had he been worrying about me?

My father held me close, giving off the impression we were hugging. "I got your message. I have the work van waiting just outside the Core gates. They wouldn't let me bring it through to the palace though."

"It'll have to do." I shook my head. "I have friends here, not many but enough to help me get out of here."

The last time I'd tried to escape had suffered from poor timing. This time, I wouldn't make the same mistake. Plus, I wouldn't have Marsha to worry about. I still didn't have my proof though. I could bring the book about converts - but that was still with Marsha. I'd have to see if he left it in his room if I could get out of mine alone.

"When should we expect you?" my father asked just as a horn blared announcing it was time for me to enter.

I didn't have a chance to answer before the double doors began to open. I moved us before the double doors, my arm looped through his, and forced a smile on my face.

The ballroom had been set up so there were two sides of chairs lined up in rows. Cutting through the middle of those rows, a long crimson carpet extended to where Patrick and the priest waited. Flower petals had been sprinkled along the pathway I would walk, and bouquets hung from the end of each row.

If this had been a real wedding, I would have had bride's maids, my stepsisters, and some female friends. Maybe even the little girl who lived next door to us back in the Glade would have been my flower girl. However, since this was not a marriage of love but of duty, those had been excluded, and in their place, unfamiliar faces and cameras zoomed in to take in everything.

The members of the Fold sat on one side of the room, while my stepfamily sat on the other. Their mixture of fake expressions made me want to throw my bouquet at their faces, just to break the façade. Everything about this whole atrocity was a sham.

Except for Patrick.

I finally allowed my eyes to look down the aisle and up to my groom's face. Dressed in a white tuxedo and his hair slicked back, I'd have found him handsome had I not wanted to stab him so much. The expression on his face didn't help matters. It wasn't that of an anxious groom or the blank slate I usually saw in public. No, instead, Patrick had a small smile on the tip of his lips which brightened as I came into view. Did he really think this was real? That I wanted to be here?

Hot fury raced through my blood at the blinding joy on his face. Through my fake smile, I said out of the corner of my mouth, "I'm not sure. We have the reception after this, and then the honeymoon. So, tomorrow night? I would think things would die down enough for me to sneak away."

"All right, I will make sure everything is prepared," my father murmured back, patting my hand. "I am so proud of you my Clarabelle."

My eyes watered as he stopped me before Patrick and the minister. I knew my father's words were toward the rebellion and not my marriage to Patrick. He didn't have the same ambitions as my stepmother, something I was thankful for every day.

"Who gives this woman to be wed?" the minister asked my father.

"Her family and I do," my father said in return. He met Patrick's eyes, and for a second, that grin faltered, but then it was back. My father turned to me, kissing my cheek before handing me over to Patrick.

Every step towards Patrick felt like nails stabbing into my feet. The grin on my lips felt like it might break my face at any second and Patrick noticed. His grip on my hand tightened to an almost painful pressure, never breaking his mask of joy.

"Dearly beloved, we are gathered here today to join this man and this woman in holy matrimony," the minister started, but I drowned him out. Most of the words being said didn't pertain to us. Patrick wasn't a man. We wouldn't love and cherish each other until death do us part. We'd more likely be the cause of each other's death - his more than mine. The sickness wouldn't matter since I was pretty sure vampires couldn't get sick, and I didn't see myself sitting at Patrick's bedside nursing him back to health.

Patrick's fingers dug into my hand jerking me out of my thoughts. My eyes jerked up to see the minister staring at me. Clearing my throat, I fumbled, "I'm sorry. Can you say that again?"

An impatient frown covered his mouth as he asked, "Do you take this man?"

I turned my gaze to Patrick, this man who had captivated me from the beginning. Someone I had thought wouldn't be so bad to end up with. That was, of course, before I found out his little issue. Even if I could look past his vampirism, what he had done to Marsha and Tillie I couldn't forgive. I'd do everything in my power to bring him and the rest of the Fold down, even if it meant marrying him.

"I do," I said, a grin on my face that I knew had to be scary from the way Patrick flinched.

He muttered out his answer to the question when asked, but his smile never returned. Before long, the ceremony was over, and it was time for him to kiss me. We couldn't skip that part like I was sure we both wanted to, the cameras and the Fold were watching too closely.

We turned toward each other, the crowd waiting with bated breath. Patrick locked eyes with me and reached up cupping me behind the head. I stared into his eyes, all my anger and hatred coming forth, making his hand curl tightly in my hair. His mouth pressed against mine in a clash of teeth that made my lip bleed. Asher released a small sound, which caused a chorus of laughs from the crowd. We must have looked like we couldn't get enough of each other the way I clung to him to keep myself from making a scene.

When it was over, we jerked away from each other with so much force I almost fell over. Patrick's hand clasped onto mine keeping me upright. The crowd cheered as we turned to them as a united front. What they didn't know was that nothing could have been further from the truth.

Chapter 18

WILLOW HAD BEEN RIGHT. I should have eaten more for breakfast.

I hadn't realized how many people wanted to congratulate me until now. People I didn't know. Even people I didn't like.

Zara hugged me. My skin still crawled because of it. I was pretty sure she was trying to dump something on my dress, but the very act itself was freaky.

To make matters worse, Patrick stayed at my side every step of the night. We cut the cake. I had been sorely tempted to brandish the cake knife as a weapon, but Patrick had seen it coming, simply taking over the cake cutting on his own.

"Cram it in her face!" a voice from the crowd shouted as we did the ritual feeding of each other. I had a feeling if this had been a vampire-only service it would be a different kind of feeding.

Against the crowd's wishes, Patrick held a small piece of cake up to my mouth, and I parted my lips. It couldn't have been more awkward if I was standing there naked for all to see. His fingertips brushed my lips, and my body remembered how I'd craved him before. Stupid blood. Why did you have to remind me now?

I'd thought I was free of his pull, but apparently, I was only pushing it down. It reared its head now, and it wasn't happy at the distance between Patrick and me.

That was easily remedied when it was time to dance. A slow song played overhead, something pretty and sultry all at once. Patrick pulled me onto the dance floor, one hand on my hip while the other held my hand. He kept a good foot between us which I'm sure seemed strange to the watching party goers, but I think he was to the point of not caring anymore. At least, I was.

"You're upset," Patrick commented a few seconds after we started to dance.

"Really?" I quirked a brow, looking anywhere but at him. "What gave it away?"

"Well, the fact that you haven't given me a genuine smile all day was a hint." Patrick's hand squeezed my waist, causing me to look back at him. "What is on your mind?"

"Besides, the obvious?"

Patrick glanced around us before twirling me and bringing me back around. This time he drew me flush against him so I couldn't ignore him if I wanted to.

His voice was low, barely a whisper as he said, "I know this is not what you dreamed your wedding would be like." I snorted, but he continued. "But Asher and I did try to make it as pleasant as possible."

"Except I have been confined to my room for the last week and only let out to be tortured by the dressmaker." I shook my head. "You really need to update your definition of pleasant because I can tell you nothing about this has been close to it."

"What would you have me do?" Patrick asked, his breath brushing my ear. "What would make you happy?"

Immediately, my answer came to my lips, "Let me go home."

The song came to an end before Patrick could answer. He led me off the dance floor and toward our table where we would be once against assaulted by well-wishers.

Patrick pulled my chair out for me, and I sat down.

As he pushed it in, he leaned in close. "Even if I wanted to, I am afraid we are both in too deep to change course now."

I twisted around to argue with him, but he had already left. I watched his back as it moved through the crowd and then disappeared altogether, leaving me alone to face the masses.

I took the moment alone to drink the champagne they had been so helpful to keep in ample supply. The bubbles fizzled as they went down, making my stomach buzz. Thankfully, I got through three glasses before my next visitor arrived.

Tris approached the table, her gown for the evening a bit scandalous for a wedding. Black sheer fabric covered her curves, and her breasts were just moments from popping out of their confines. But it wasn't her outfit that shocked me so much as it was the man on her arm.

"Marsha," I gasped, standing up so fast I knocked my glass over, spilling champagne all over the table. A servant quickly stepped in to clean it up before it ruined my dress. Not that I cared, my attention was solely focused on the man in front of me.

"Congratulations are in order," Tris purred as she stood before me, her hand stroking up and down Marsha's tuxedo-clad arm. "I have to say I am quite overjoyed to see our Patrick finally settling down. We were beginning to worry."

I ignored Tris's attempt at conversation and stared at Marsha, looking for some semblance of recognition in his eyes. His brown eyes stared at me, a pleasant expression on his face but nothing like the way he used to look at me.

"You know it is unbecoming of the bride to ogle someone else's partner at her own reception." Tris scowled. "What will people say?"

"What did you do to him?" I snapped, finally giving her the full weight of my glare.

Tris's lip curled into a wicked grin. "Exactly what we promised. Marsha does not remember anything before arriving. He knows he has won the election and has become my beau for however long I see fit. And he's just fine with it. Aren't you, dear?"

She trailed her fingertips along the front of Marsha's shirt, and for the first time since seeing him, Marsha responded. He looked down at Tris with adoration and desire, a smile on his face as if he were in a dream.

This wasn't right. This wasn't what they said would happen. He wasn't even the same person anymore. They'd made him into nothing more than a puppet for Tris's amusement.

My anger was getting the better of me, and I prepared myself to launch myself across the table, wedding be damned. Before I could even get one foot up, two hands wrapped around my waist and jerked me back into my seat. Patrick sat down beside me, his hand tight on my thigh.

"I think you've had a bit too much to drink." Patrick laughed, causing the onlookers - who I hadn't even noticed - to dissipate.

I glared at Tris who didn't seem fazed in the slightest. Searching for the knife on the table, my hand shot out to grab it, but Patrick was faster. He snatched it up, setting it on the other side of his plate. I turned my anger to him, needing to draw blood somewhere.

"You've destroyed him," I accused. "This isn't what you said would happen. He's nothing more than a puppet for her to use and discard."

Patrick turned his eyes from me to focus on Tris. "We have done what we said with a few extra tweaks. Now, Tris will get the full benefits of having a partner who wants to be by her side and isn't distracted by past acquaintances. As it should be."

A smug grin spread across Tris's face, and I jerked in my seat once more. If it hadn't been for Patrick's hand, I would have clawed her face off. Patrick waved Tris away. She quickly led Marsha from the table and toward the dance floor where she plastered herself against him.

"It isn't enough that I had to marry you. You feel like you have to torture me now?" I growled, turning my gaze back to Patrick.

"It wasn't my idea."

"Then you should have stopped it," I countered, crossing my arms over my chest with a huff. "Or is this one of those occasions where you were outvoted?"

"It was, and you should be thankful for it." The warning in Patrick's tone set me on edge. "What they wanted to do instead would have made this night far worse."

"I don't see how that's possible," I muttered.

Patrick replied with, "Just wait, it will."

Patrick's words caused my anxiety to soar. Paranoid, I jumped at every person who came to talk to me and felt as if I might throw up at any moment. My new husband wasn't of any help, he didn't speak to me more than he had to and kept leaving the table to do God knew what before coming back with an even grimmer expression on his face.

Eventually, though, the night was coming to an end which meant I could finally relax. The majority of the guests including my family had left for their homes, leaving only the Fold members left. That should have been a warning.

Marcus and Beaford stepped toward the table, their grins too happy to be good. Patrick stood by my side and offered me his hand. I took it against my better judgment and let him lead me around the table.

He stopped a few feet from Beaford and Marcus. "The night has come to an end, and as per our ruling before, after this night, Clarabelle is no longer under watch and confined to her room."

"Wait, what?" My brow furrowed as I shot a look at Patrick. "I thought it was until I converted?"

Patrick wouldn't look at me. I turned my eyes from him and toward the rest of the room. Each Fold member had a matching smirk on their face as if they knew something I didn't.

"Dear girl," Beaford chuckled, stepping closer to me, Marcus matching his steps. "Don't you get it?"

I shook my head as if somehow it would make him stop saying what I feared he might say.

"Your wedding night will also be your last night as a human and your first step toward conversion," Marcus finished for Beaford. Before I could completely process his words, he and Beaford grabbed me.

I screamed and clawed at them, demanding them to let me go. I even yelled for Patrick to save me, but he just stared straight forward as if he couldn't hear me. They dragged me out of the ballroom, kicking and screaming. Someone must have thought I was making too much of a commotion because a sharp pain started in my head and my vision began to blur.

The last thing I saw before the world darkened around me was the closing of the ballroom doors, signaling the end of my humanity and the beginning of the end.

Chapter 19

WHEN I AWOKE AGAIN, the room was dark. I tried to sit up, but I couldn't lift my upper body. My arms were tied down. I tried to move my legs, but they wouldn't budge.

I searched around me but only found darkness. I screamed, hoping someone would hear me. All it did was intensify the pounding already thrumming in my head.

Settling back down, the cool surface beneath me making me think my bed was made of concrete or metal. I closed my eyes, and I tried to calm myself. Where could they have taken me? The last thing I remembered was Patrick announcing something about - my eyes flashed opened - the conversion.

Beaford and Marcus had taken me. Someone had knocked me out. Then I woke up here. But if this is supposed to be where they were going to convert me, where was everyone?

Or had they already converted me? Was I a vampire?

My heart raced as I stuck my tongue up to feel my teeth. No fangs. I relaxed slightly. So, it hadn't happened yet.

A dim light flicked on, and a soft melody began to play from somewhere on my left. I searched the room until my eyes fell on a chair in the corner where Patrick sat.

He had discarded his suit jacket and unbuttoned his cuffs as well as the first two buttons of his shirt. His pale eyes watched me from where he sat, his expression too neutral for me to make out what he was planning.

I struggled against my restraints and demanded, "Let me go. We didn't agree to this."

"I know. I'm sorry." Patrick shook his head, and for a moment, I believed he actually was sorry. "I hadn't wanted to do it this way. If I could have left it up to you, I would have, but they forced my hand."

"Who did? Why?"

Patrick met my gaze. "You know who. The Fold found my punishment of you too lax, and there was talk of appointing a new leader. Someone who had more of a backbone."

"But they can't!" I argued. "You're their leader. They fear you."

Patrick smiled and not a happy one. "Only because they must. If they truly wished to replace me, they could. Which is why I have to make compromises."

"And I'm one of those compromises?" I spat. "Marsha? Tillie? Were they compromises too?"

Patrick's expression hardened. "You have to understand the position I'm in."

"No, I don't."

"If you and that boy hadn't tried to escape, I wouldn't have been forced to do this. In all honesty, you brought this on yourself." Patrick locked eyes with me.

"Bull crap." I jerked up as far as the restraints allowed me. "You are doing what is best for you. I'm only an afterthought."

"Now, dear wife," - Patrick grinned - "you were always in the forefront of my mind. I would never do anything to hurt you if I had a choice."

"You do. You can let me go."

Patrick stood from the chair and approached me. "It's far too late for that. You should be happy it is me doing the conversion. Marcus had almost gotten them to approve his bid to do it. He seems quite taken with you."

"Then why didn't you let him?" I shifted away from Patrick as he brushed against the table. I didn't want to be anywhere near him. The very sight of him disgusted me.

"Because he would have made it a game. Toyed with you for hours before finally taking you. You'd lose your mind before you changed, and you would have been no use to anyone then."

"Is that all I am to you?" I stared up into his eyes, searching for some weakness in him to exploit. "Just a tool to get what you want?"

"It would be easier if you were." Patrick slid a finger down the side of my arm. It was then I realized the lace of my wedding gown had been ripped away, leaving me in just the slip beneath. At least, I wasn't naked.

"Pity, they destroyed your gown," Patrick mused, his touch causing goose bumps on my skin. "It was such a lovely creation. Asher will be so distraught."

"Asher," I said, grasping at whatever I could. "Where is he? Does he know what you are doing?"

Patrick's ashamed expression was all the answer I needed.

"He doesn't, does he?" I accused, gaping at him. "What are you going to tell him when he finds out? Will you say you had no choice? You were forced to?" The words curdled in my mouth like spoiled milk.

Clearing his throat, Patrick dropped his hand. "Asher knows what has to be done." He moved away from me and started to unbutton his shirt.

"What ... what are you doing?" I gasped, pulling on my restraints.

"I don't wish to get blood on this shirt," Patrick explained as if it were the most natural thing in the world. "It's hard to get out."

When he draped his shirt over the chair, he turned back to me. "I want you to know that this will bring me no pleasure."

"Yeah, right," I said, dryly.

"It won't," Patrick countered, stopping next to me once more. "It's good you have experienced this before because it will be like the first time I tasted you."

I squirmed on the table. The part of me I had buried became excited, eager to have his fangs in me once again. The other half of me caused me to flinch away as he reached for me.

"I'm going to untie you now," Patrick explained, his hands on my arms. "But if you fight, I will be forced to restrain you."

I nodded my consent, though I was thinking something else entirely. The moment he undid my binds, I attacked. Scratching and biting, I did everything I could to get away from him, but he was too strong.

He grabbed me by the back of my hair, arching my neck to the side. "I am truly sorry."

I opened my mouth to tell him how sorry I thought he was, but before I could get a word out, he struck. His fangs pierced the side of my neck and the euphoria from the first time came rushing back with a vengeance.

Suddenly, the hands trying to push him away dragged him closer. A gurgling groan ripped from my throat as he drank from me. My body heat rose, and I felt like I was wearing too many clothes. I tried to pull on them, but Patrick trapped my hands, keeping them against his chest.

Unlike the last time he had fed on me, there was no Marsha to stop him, no one around to interrupt us. He drank for what felt like an eternity, and the pleasure that came with his bite started to fade, and my body started to sag. My breaths came out in pants now, and my arms were too heavy to keep up.

Patrick laid me back down on the table, my eyes fluttering open and closed. I barely noticed when his fangs retracted from my neck as he leaned away from me. I watched through heavy lids as Patrick brought his own wrist to his mouth and bit down. Blood poured from the wound, and he pressed it to my mouth.

I kept my mouth closed, not wanting what he was offering me. My head still screamed for his bite, but I had enough sense left to know nothing good would come of me drinking his blood.

Patrick used his other hand to grip my jaw and put enough force on it to force it open. Before I could close it, he shoved his wrist into my mouth. Hot blood touched my tongue, and it filled my mouth forcing me to swallow or choke on it.

It dripped down my throat and at first, my stomach fought against it. Then as if it knew something I didn't, it accepted it. Craved it even. Renewed energy filled me, and I gripped onto Patrick's wrist holding it close to me.

Finally, when my stomach said enough, I shoved his arm away. My heart raced as I felt something happening. His blood was doing something to me. Changing me.

Patrick's presence moved away, but I didn't care. My chest beat rapidly, and an ache started from the center spreading out to the rest of my body until I felt like one massive bruise.

I cried out as a stinging pain shot through my gums. Something slithered through the veins, and I felt the hardened lengths of my new fangs push against my lips. Tears streamed down my face as the despair of what was happening to me morphed into hunger.

That overwhelming thirst made me jerk up from the table. I stared down at myself, expecting to see some kind of monster in my place, but besides the fangs, my body had remained the same. Only the insides had changed.

I shook my head as I fought the hunger inside of me and the anguish began to settle in. It'd happened, the one thing I had promised never to let them do to me, and I had barely struggled.

My eyes turned to Patrick who watched me with a cursory gaze. I hated him. Hated him for bringing me here and for doing this to me. However, my hatred for him would never be as bad as how much I hated myself.

Chapter 20

WHEN PATRICK FINALLY LET me out of the basement, I discovered it was still the night of the wedding. My conversion had taken up a total of a few hours.

I felt like it should have taken longer. How does one's body get used to it in such a brief time? My skin tingled and itched as if I didn't belong in my own skin anymore. The light from the hallway burned my eyes, and I had to stare down at the ground just to see.

Patrick tried to take my arm as he led me back to my room, but I jerked away from his touch. "Don't touch me. Don't ever touch me again." My voice came out gravelly, but I didn't care, just as long as he stayed away from me.

As we made our way back to my room, I was surprised that we hadn't run into anyone. I still wore my slip, and the blood from Patrick still coated my face. It felt sticky and tight, pulling at my lips each time I moved them.

"Here," Patrick reached for me again but dropped his hand, a disheartened look on his face. He opened a door leading into a bathroom.

I walked in and shut the door behind me, leaving Patrick in the hallway. I didn't glance in the mirror as I splashed my face with water, rubbing my skin until the water came away clear. Drying my face, I slowly lowered it.

Meeting my gaze in the mirror, I scowled. I wanted it to be different. I needed it to be different. I shouldn't look the same. The monster I was should have been as easy to see as I felt on the inside.

Throwing the towel into the sink, I stomped out of the bathroom. Patrick stood there with a robe. Where he had retrieved it from, I didn't know or care. I bypassed him and the robe and marched down the hallway.

What was a little skin in the grand aspect of things? I was a monster. A blood-sucking fiend. If I wanted to strut around naked now, I would. After all, any humans who remembered it would be dead long before me.

"Clarabelle," Patrick shouted after me, his footstep pounding on the tile floor as he caught up with. Ignoring his call, I made my feet move faster. I didn't want to talk. I didn't want to see his face. The hunger inside was barely contained by the rage boiling in my blood.

I made it to my bedroom door with Patrick still on my heels. I darted inside before he could catch me and slammed the door shut behind me. Locking it, I backed away from the door. Part of me expected him to come bursting through at any moment. When his footsteps stopped in front of it but no further, I held my breath. He stood there for a moment, but then he left. A door opened and shut down the hallway, and I knew he wouldn't come back.

Stripping myself of my clothes, I hurried into the bathroom. I turned the water up as hot as it would go and got in. Scrubbing at my skin, I rubbed until it began to hurt. Dirty. I still felt so dirty. It was like something was inside of me, and I couldn't get it out as much as I tried.

I didn't climb out of the shower until the water turned cold, and when I did, I didn't bother drying off. I walked into the bedroom and crawled into bed. I buried myself in the blankets and cried. I cried until I had no more tears to give and then I sank into a dreamless sleep.

When I woke, it was still dark outside, and my stomach screamed. Hunger burned in my throat, and I couldn't stay in bed any longer. One glance at the clock told me it was no longer the early hours of the morning but night time again. I'd slept all day.

I searched the room for clothes. Once I was dressed, I started for the door. I needed to feed. Anything to get the burning to stop.

Opening the door, I almost stepped on Asher laying on the floor. Backing up, I bumped him with my foot. Asher shifted and then his eyes fluttered open. When they focused in on me, he jumped to his feet.

"Clara," Asher gasped and wrapped me in his arms. I let him, even though my body still ached. "I didn't know." He cried into my hair. "I didn't know."

I patted his back, my eyes brimming with tears I didn't think I even had left. "I know," I murmured.

"Are you okay?" Asher pulled away, looking me over. "He didn't hurt you, did he?"

I shook my head. "Not any more than he had to." I had said that to make Asher feel better, but as I recalled what happened, it was true. Patrick had only done what he said he would. From the way he explained it, someone else would have made it even worse.

Still didn't make it right.

"Let's go inside." Asher ushered me back into my room and closed the door. "How do you feel? Can I get you anything? I know I felt a bit disoriented when I first changed."

I frowned, and my hand went to my stomach.

Asher's eyes lit up. "Oh, you're hungry. Of course, you would be." He fumbled for his words and snapped his fingers. "I can bring you to the feeding room."

I shot him a look.

"Wait no, not that." Asher shook his head. "I know, I've got just the thing. Hold on, I'll be back."

Asher left the room. Not sure when he'd come back, I sat by the window. My eyes could easily see through the darkness of the courtyard. What had previously been dark shadows, I could now see plain as day, and what had once been too far away to see was as clear as if it was right in front of me.

I caught sight of something just beyond the palace walls. A familiar van top that I had seen all my life.

Father. He was still waiting for me. He didn't know what had happened. Of course, he didn't. They would have made sure he was out of the palace before they converted me.

I stood from my seat and headed for the door. The need to leave thrummed in my blood, my hunger barely a nuisance.

When I opened the door, Asher was there, just about to knock. In his hand, he had a steaming cup. A coppery scent wafted up from the cup, and my hunger roared back to life. Without asking, I grabbed the cup from his hands and brought it to my lips.

"Careful," Asher warned, but I didn't listen pouring the hot liquid into my mouth and burning my tongue. "It's hot."

I swallowed painfully and then took another tentative drink.

Asher smiled at me. "A bit hungry, are we?"

"A bit." The edge of my lip tipped up and then fell when I realized the blood had to have come from somewhere.

"Don't worry," Asher said as if reading my mind. "I got it from someone willing. No mind wiping needed."

Still staring down at the cup, I wondered if it was one of the girls. My stomach growled, and I couldn't override it with my guilt. I tipped the rest of the cup's contents into my mouth and swallowed every drop.

I grimaced and handed the cup back to Asher, who laughed.

"Don't worry, you get used to it."

"I doubt it."

We stood there in an awkward silence. Eventually, Asher broke it. "You've been asleep all day. I was worried something had gone wrong."

"I was tired." I shrugged.

"I'd imagine so." Asher shifted in place. "Do you want to go for a walk? Or I could get you something else to eat?" I made a face, and he quickly added, "Real food, I promise."

I shook my head. "I'd rather just go back to bed, to be honest."

"Oh." Asher's face fell. "Okay. I understand. It's a lot to deal with. You probably want to be alone."

"Yeah."

Asher moved toward the door. "Well, if you need anything let me know. I'll be around. They can't let humans serve you right now because of the ..." He trailed off.

"I might eat them?" I offered with a bitter grin.

"Yeah, that." Asher sighed. "Anyway, I'll be in Patrick's office if you need me."

I nodded, not trusting myself to say anything else. The only thought in my mind was getting out of here and to my father. The longer Asher was here, the more likely I would blab my intentions.

Asher left, and I waited a good ten minutes before I headed for the door again. Opening it slowly, I peeked out into the hallway. No one was coming, good.

Slipping out of my room, I closed it, trying to make as little noise as possible. I had to pass Patrick's room and office to get out of the hallway, so I tiptoed in front of the two doors until I was clear. Then I quickened my pace until I was almost running.

I passed a few servants, and a smell caught my attention. I slowed my pace and glanced back. My eyes locked onto one of the servant girl's necks and my feet were suddenly moving toward it.

"Miss?" the girl's voice broke whatever trance I had been in, and I shook my head.

"I ... uh ... sorry," I muttered and then forced myself to turn back around. My stomach yelled at me for it, but I ignored it, shoving the feeling deep down inside of me.

I passed a few more humans but didn't stop. I kept moving until I was outside. The night air cleared my lungs, making the hunger just a bit more bearable.

Turning toward where I'd seen my father's van, I moved faster than I'd ever done before. Patrick had said they weren't fast, but perhaps he didn't remember what it is like to be human. I zipped across the lawn, my speed causing my own little breeze pulling my hair and whipping at my clothes. In no time at all – literally – I was in one spot and then the other before I could even finish processing my movements.

I stared up at the stone wall, trying to figure out how I was going to get over it. I'd never been much of a climber; my upper body strength mainly came from pulling weeds and cutting down the harvest. We had other stronger people to do the heavy lifting.

But you're stronger now, a voice reminded me.

Oh, yeah. The only snippet of information Patrick had been forthcoming about.

Still doubtful, I slowly reached up and grabbed hold of the side of one of the stones. When I easily lifted myself up, a small part of me marveled at my newfound strength. Letting myself enjoy this little bit, I grappled up the wall until I sat on top with freedom only a hair's breath away.

I didn't stop to glance back at the palace, the place I once stood in awe of. Now, all it represented to me was pain and heartache. I had no intentions of going back unless it was to pull it down, brick by brick.

Staring down the other side of the wall, the part of me that still thought it was human cringed at the height. If I was still an ordinary human, the fall would probably break my leg.

But you're not human anymore, that annoying voice reminded me.

Holding my breath, I swung my leg over the other side and tried not to think too much about broken bones as I dropped off the wall. I landed on the other side of the wall in a crouch. I'd barely made a sound.

And hadn't broken anything, I grinned to myself before frowning.

It felt wrong somehow to like the new abilities that had been forced upon me. However, those powers were what made it possible for me to escape, something I wouldn't have been able to do on my own. The irony of it didn't go unnoticed.

I'd only just stood from my crouch when someone jumped from the van. My muscled tensed, getting ready to run in case I had been wrong, and this wasn't my father's van. The person rounded the vehicle, and the moment I saw my father's tired face, I relaxed.

"Clarabelle," my father gasped when he saw me. "What happened to you?"

"Nothing," I shook my head, forcing my hunger back as the scent of my father penetrated my senses. "It's just been a long night."

Whether or not my father believed me, he nodded and helped me into the truck. I climbed into the back where they stored the goods and ducked behind a stack of wheat bags.

The van shook as we made our way down the road, bumping me against the walls. It was hard to believe it had only been a few weeks since I had come to the Core. So much had happened. Friends gained and lost. Enemies made, and I'd even gotten married. It seemed like a dream, a horrible, nightmare I couldn't wake up from.

A sob burst from my lips before I could stop it and I covered my mouth with my hand. Tears burned in lines down my face as I realized I might never see any of them again. I'd never see Marsha again. Not that he would care since he didn't remember me.

At least, I had accomplished something. I had gotten away, just like Marsha had wanted. I could rally the people and show them what kind of monsters they were dealing with. After all, I was all the proof they needed.

About the Author

Erin Bedford is an otaku, recovering coffee addict, and Legend of Zelda fanatic. Her brain is so full of stories that need to be told that she must get them out or explode into a million screaming chibis. Obsessed with fairy tales and bad boys, she hasn't found a story she can't twist to match her deviant mind full of innuendos, snarky humor, and dream guys.

On the outside, she's a work from home mom and bookbinger. One the inside, she's a thirteen-year-old boy screaming to get out and tell you the pervy joke they found online. As an ex-computer programmer, she dreams of one day combining her love for writing and college credits to make the ultimate video game!

Until then, when she's not writing, Erin is devouring as many books as possible on her quest to have the biggest book gut of all time. She's written over thirty books, ranging from paranormal romance, urban fantasy, and even scifi romance.

Come chat me up!
www.erinbedford.com
Facebook.com/erinrbedford
twitter.com/erin_bedford
Don't forget to follow me on Goodreads, Pinterest, Instagram, and YouTube!

Want to be the first to know about my new releases?
Erinbedford.com/newsletter